PLAYER VS PLAYER

ULTIMATE GAMING SHOWDOWN

START GAME

THE HUB MAP

GAME MANUAL

AFFINITIES AND TEKNIKS

PLAYER VS PLAYER

ULTIMATE GAMING SHOWDOWN

BOOK 1

M. K. ENGLAND

RANDOM HOUSE 🏠 NEW YORK

Text copyright © 2022 by Random House Children's Books
Cover art copyright © 2022 by Pablo Ballesteros
Interior art copyright © 2022 by Chris Danger

All rights reserved. Published in the United States by Random House Children's Books, a division of Penguin Random House LLC, New York.

Random House and the colophon are registered trademarks of Penguin Random House LLC.

Visit us on the Web! rhcbooks.com

Educators and librarians, for a variety of teaching tools, visit us at RHTeachersLibrarians.com

Library of Congress Cataloging-in-Publication Data
Names: England, M. K., author. | Danger, Chris, illustrator.
Title: Ultimate gaming showdown / M. K. England; art by Chris Danger.
Description: First edition. | New York: Random House Children's Books, 2022. |
Series: Player vs. player; 1
Summary: A virtual tournament is announced in *Affinity,* the biggest online multiplayer video game in the world, and four kids are invited to compete for the grand prize—and a chance to become a professional gamer.
Identifiers: LCCN 2021023952 (print) | LCCN 2021023953 (ebook) |
ISBN 978-0-593-43340-9 (trade) | ISBN 978-0-593-43341-6 (lib. bdg.) |
ISBN 978-0-593-43342-3 (ebook)
Subjects: CYAC: Video games—Fiction. | Artificial intelligence—Fiction. |
Online identities—Fiction. | Friendship—Fiction. | LCGFT: Novels.
Classification: LCC PZ7.1.E536 UI 2022 (print) | LCC PZ7.1.E536 (ebook) |
DDC [Fic]—dc23

Printed in the United States of America
10 9 8 7 6 5 4 3 2 1
First Edition

To N:

This one's for you.

The couple that games together stays together.

And for our little Player 3, too.

Welcome to the world, baby.

SAVE GAME

THE HUB MAP

GAME MANUAL

AFFINITIES AND TEKNIKS

JOSH

I know it's my job to get punched in the face repeatedly, but this?

This is the *worst*.

All the color bleeds out of the screen as my character drops his shield and falls to his knees with an exaggerated groan. For the *third time* in less than a minute. Just in case I missed what happened, I'm helpfully reminded in big red letters:

ELIMINATED by Viperzz!

The game spins the camera around so I can see from every angle as Viperzz jumps repeatedly on my fallen avatar's face. I designed it to look similar to my own, since the game had enough character options for me to get pretty close to "skinny Chinese kid with glasses." Regretting that decision now. Two of my own teammates charge onto the screen and join in the stomping of my too-real-looking face before finally attacking our enemy like they're supposed to. Somehow, in between slinging arrows of electricity at the other team and trying not to die, my so-called teammates still manage to type out some trash talk.

[Team Chat]

StryderX: Get good, you **DELIGHTFUL UNICORN OF SUNSHINE**

OohShinee: Try staying alive for more than ten seconds, **SUPER NINJA**

I roll my eyes and hit the F12 key to take a screenshot. **DELIGHTFUL UNICORN OF SUNSHINE** is a pretty good one. Within a week of getting this game, I downloaded a mod that turns common insults and whining into something much more fun, and I haven't turned it off since. Things slip through the filter once in a while, but at least it makes match chat only mildly annoying instead of a vast ocean of school-lunch vomit that makes me sad for the whole human species.

And sometimes the filter's random positivity makes for some really funny screenshots. I still have the shot of the time some random guy's string of insults ended up telling me I was a **FLUFFY PIRATE CHEETAH OF JOY** who could go **CELEBRATE** myself like a **PRO ASTRONAUT**.

There's no filter in the world that makes voice chat tolerable, though. Forget that.

My two "teammates" run off just as my respawn timer

counts down to zero. I appear back at my team's starting point at full health, ready to try again.

Whoo.

I shake out my hands and resettle them on the WASD keys and mouse. I really do *try* not to let it get to me. Those other two are sticking together for a reason. They're probably friends who play together after school, just like I'm doing . . . but by myself. Because we had to move for my mom's job *yet again,* for the third time since I started middle school. Maybe I'd be like them if I had someone to play with, too.

Then they charge headfirst together into a giant, obvious net of stun traps set by the other team, leading to their quick and ugly demise.

Never mind. There is no universe where I could ever be like them. Even my dog, Marvin, would be a better gamer buddy than these guys, and all he does is sleep on my feet and fart in the middle of every match. His stink instantly turns every battle into Hard Mode.

If I can't have someone to game with after school, though, at least I can be the top-ranked *Affinity* player in my role. I'm a tank, and it's my job to take the hits and keep others safe so they can do their own jobs: healing, attacking up close, or attacking from long range. No matter how bad these two guys are, it is my duty: I will protect them from their own stupidity.

Or try to, I guess, because there they go again, walking headfirst into the other team's clutches without my backup. Our other teammate, who's been totally silent, is attempting to follow along with their "strategy," but they're clearly ignoring her. All three of them get destroyed before I have a chance to catch up and protect them.

> **StryderX:** Uuuuugh, we are getting
>   completely owned
>
> **OohShinee:** Why are you two so bad?

Yeah, 'cause *we're* the bad ones. Normally I don't bother with jerks like these. They never listen, and they'll never change. They're like bullies at school: anything you throw at them will just get used against you five seconds later. Fighting back only drags the whole thing out.

Maybe it's the miserable day I had at school, or maybe it's the four matches I played right before this one that all had teams just as selfish. But this time I can't let it go. I do the thing I *never* do, and type furiously into team chat while waiting to respawn again.

> **TankasaurusRex:** Maybe if we actually
>   had a team of four in this match
>   instead of two bestest buddies ever
>   skipping around alone together, we
>   might walk out with a win.
>
> **TankasaurusRex:** We could, you know,
>   actually try to play *together.*

Pointless, though.

> **OohShinee:** DANCE off, **SPACE CHAMPION**
>
> **StryderX:** You can't keep up with us

Should have known better.

The match timer ticks down—five minutes to go. I can deal with these guys for five more minutes, take the loss, and move on with my life. It won't hurt my ranking that badly.

Then a private message pops up in my chat window.

> **[Private Message]**
>
> **PunchyTime:** Ha, nice
>
> **PunchyTime:** We could work together and make this a 4 vs 2+2 match, at least.
>
> **PunchyTime:** Assuming these two noobs don't rage quit on us first. This other team isn't even good. We can take them.

I check the party list, and sure enough, PunchyTime is my silent fourth teammate. She's our melee DPS—the short-range damage dealer—and I like this person *instantly*. Her character is weird. Like mine.

In *Affinity*, you can customize your character in a thousand small ways, but everyone makes the same two major choices at the start: your affinity, which is where your character gets their power, and your teknik, which is your style of fighting. There are ten Affinities, from magic runes to nature, demons to nanobots. For your teknik, you choose from twelve more selections, like sword knight, martial artist, hacker, sorcerer, or whatever else. There are over a hundred possible combinations, but like every other game in the world, people have decided that certain combos are the "right" ones. You don't see many players who don't use one of those popular builds.

Except me. I watch more Let's Play videos on YouTube than anyone, but I don't want some streamer to tell me how I should play the game. I want to *play* it, my way. I'm a Rune Knight, the least popular tank build.

PunchyTime apparently agrees. Her class combo shows up as Demon Puncher . . . which I have literally never seen in any match, ever.

This could be fun.

TankasaurusRex: Meet me at the gravity bridge. Let's destroy these guys.

PunchyTime: I am SO excited right now, you don't even know

My character respawns at the beginning again, standing proud in his shining silver armor, and I launch myself off the starting platform without a second to waste. This match is a "storm the castle" sort of game, but the castle we have to claim for our own is a spaceship that will let our team escape a moon base that's exploding under our feet as we go. Whichever team reaches the ship and defends it for one minute while it prepares to launch will win the match. I've played it a hundred times. I know we can win. Even with *this* team.

I see the glow of PunchyTime's demon energy before I actually set eyes on her avatar. My footsteps clang on the metal deck of the moon station as bursts of purple fire explode from around the next corner. I pull up my shield, glowing with a magical Rune of Protection, and launch myself around the corner, straight into a raging battle.

The gravity bridge is a long, thin walkway that stretches over a giant crater. Minor complication: the gravity occasionally flickers out, sending everyone floating in midbattle. That's not the most fun part, though. With a flash of blue-green light, my shield launches from my grip . . .

. . . and soars straight into the face of the girl trying to take out PunchyTime. She flies off the bridge with a comical shout, and my shield slams back into my hand as if pulled back by the world's strongest magnet. I *love* that move.

PunchyTime executes a lightning-fast roundhouse kick to another guy, and just like that, the bridge is clear. She casts a quick flash of a spell—a speed boost—and we're off, racing side by side toward the objective.

> **PunchyTime:** LOVE IT
>
> **PunchyTime:** You know how to wreck
> some face

I grin. Is there any better compliment? This total trash fire of a match has completely turned around. I tap out a quick reply:

> **TankasaurusRex:** It's an honor to punt
> fools off a bridge with you.
>
> **TankasaurusRex:** Now let's steal a
> spaceship and win this match.

JOSH

The moon base falls apart around us, raining debris and fire as we run. The other team attempts an ambush during one of the big explosions, but it's a common strategy no one actually falls for anymore. We take them out easily and push onward. At some point, our other two teammates catch up with us, silent and focused.

No one's laughing or trash talking now. Not with the shuttle—and a potential win—in sight. I can feel it in my gut. We're close.

Knock knock knock.

"Josh?"

No, not now! I think at the door, like I can telepathically keep my dad from opening it. At my feet, Marvin sits up and growls. We're finally turning this match around. I can't leave! PunchyTime lands a crushing blow that glows purple with demon magic, clearing the way to the final stretch of the map between us and the escape shuttle. All four of us run together, as a team, dodging collapsing bits of roof.

The shuttle ramp descends, waiting to welcome us aboard. We're *so close*.

Then the other team comes charging on-screen.

Knock knock knock.

"Josh, dinner. Open up."

"I'll be down in a few minutes, Dad," I say, trying to sound bored, like it's no big deal. Like I'm doing homework or something. Maybe I'll get lucky. Maybe he won't open the door. If he sees what I'm doing, why I'm stalling, it's gonna turn into a fight.

But I'm never lucky.

The door pops open, and my dad pokes his head into the room. Even from the corner of my eye, I can see how his whole body language changes.

"Josh, turn that off and get downstairs right now. Dinner is on the table."

The laser force of his disapproval hits at the same time as a fresh onslaught from the other team, and my brain struggles to balance the two. Dodge the fireball, protect PunchyTime as she crushes the opposing healer, come up with *something* to put Dad off for a few minutes.

He just doesn't get it. There are people relying on me.

These are timed team matches and I can't just walk away in the middle of it without letting everyone down. Not that it stops most people from dropping midmatch, but I like to think I'm not like most players.

"Josh, hit pause right now and be at the table in thirty seconds."

I slam my finger repeatedly on the key to keep a protective bubble up around my team as we take the shuttle, then throw myself in front of a laser blast intended for StryderX. The shuttle countdown starts. Gotta save the others, gotta take the hits and buy them time. Gotta buy *myself* some time. My dad loves to ramble on about responsibility to your family and community, and this *is* my community, so maybe . . .

"Dad, there's no pause in this game. This is happening live, and these are real people I'm protecting. If I leave now, the whole team loses. It's my responsibility to at least finish out the match. There are only two more minutes left on the timer, and I *promise* I'll be down as soon as it's over."

I risk a quick glance away from the screen to see my dad's reaction, just in time to catch the *SLAM* of the door as he storms away. Not good . . . but that's a problem for Later Josh.

Right Now Josh has a shuttle to capture.

"Thirty seconds to Blue Team liftoff," the voice-over intones, and my heart pounds hard against my ribs. Only thirty seconds until victory is ours. We're so close, and the other team knows it. With far more coordination than our team has shown so far, they meet up at the bottom of the shuttle ramp . . . then charge as one.

I can't let them on board this ship.

The voice begins the final countdown and the shuttle rumbles to life as I meet the other team head-on. I slam my shield into their tank, knocking her off the side of the ramp, then swing around to throw a magical wall up between our two teams. They turn their weapons and magic on me, but it's no use.

This is what I do. This is my kind of fight.

I absorb or deflect blow after blow, my shield flashing bright white with each hit. PunchyTime bounces around like some kind of demon rabbit, leaping from one enemy to another to interrupt their attacks before they can hurt us. OohShinee has actually decided to do his duty as healer, too. A bright green flurry of healing leaves rains down over our team, each leaf mending the damage done to us. Arrows and spells zing through the air, swords and fists fly, and the voice-over counts down ever closer to our win.

TEN! NINE! EIGHT!

StryderX flies backward, a bright bolt of electricity shorting out his nanotech armor. He falls to the ground.

SEVEN! SIX! FIVE!

PunchyTime throws herself at the other team's healer, fists wreathed in purple fire.

14

FOUR! THREE! TWO! ONE!
BLUE TEAM: VICTORY!

The words splash across the screen in bright letters as the shuttle lifts off. Our team is carried to safety just as the moon base crumbles with a final *BOOM* that makes the whole screen shake. I suck in a deep breath and shake out my hands with a wide grin.

We won.

Despite that awful start, we actually won!

I can't believe it.

The match stats display over a faded-out version of the *Affinity* logo, and I grab a quick screenshot before the image times out.

"Yessss," I hiss, pumping both fists into the air, then quickly putting them back down. My dad definitely wouldn't approve or understand, but even he can't kill my good mood now. Terrible teammates or not, I am now the number six tank in the entire game.

The. Entire. Game.

Top five, I'm coming for you.

[Private Message]

PunchyTime: Nice work, T. Thanks for the match.

TankasaurusRex: We made a pretty good team.

> **TankasaurusRex:** Well, you and me, at least.
>
> **PunchyTime:** Yeah, we should group up again sometime.

That would be *awesome*. Maybe Marvin the Farting Dog won't be my only gaming friend forever, after all.

The stats disappear as the screen fills with a still image of the Hub, the zone where players hang out between matches. At the bottom, a loading bar fills little by little until the image disappears, replaced by the real thing.

The Hub is set up like a huge pie with different slices themed for each of the ten Affinities. There's a forested area for the nature types, a futuristic neon cityscape for the nanotechs, and so on. You can buy houses and apartments, get new gear, change your character's appearance, and just hang out with other players. In the center of the pie is an enormous gathering area with a center stage that is often taken over by people dueling or showing off their shiny new armor.

Today, the center stage is surrounded by a humongous party in progress. As soon as my character finishes loading into the Hub, a system-wide message takes over my chat window:

I have to miss it.

Agh, the suspense is *killing* me. I think I can call myself a top player, being the number six tank in the game (which I will never get tired of saying). What is this opportunity they're teasing? Besides that, *Affinity* events are always over-the-top awesome, with real-world bands playing in game and exclusive gifts for the players who attend. I've missed every single one since the game was released.

PunchyTime: You sticking around for the announcement? I'm so curious.

> **TankasaurusRex:** I want to so bad,
> but I have to go eat dinner or my
> parents will throw my computer off
> the roof and leave its guts for the
> vultures.

I'm kidding. I think.

> **TankasaurusRex:** Will you tell me what
> the event is like?
> **TankasaurusRex:** I'll be on tomorrow
> morning before school.

Then, with my breath held, I click the Add Friend button.

It takes thirty eternal seconds for the reply to appear. I stare at the door to my bedroom, willing my dad to wait just *one more minute.*

> PUNCHYTIME HAS ACCEPTED YOUR FRIEND REQUEST.
>
> **PunchyTime:** Yeah, I'll be on. I'll tell
> you all about it.

I shake out the fist I'd been nervously clenching and hit the O key to open up my friends list.

Friends List (1 online)
PunchyTime

TankasaurusRex: Thanks. Talk to you tomorrow.

Maybe. Possibly. Could be that Punchy will never talk to me again after tonight.

But maybe not. Maybe we'll play another match tomorrow. Maybe the next day, too. Maybe I'll finally have someone to play with after school, like those two guys on our team earlier. But, you know, not awful.

I can dream, right?

The sound of clanging dishes and a spicy smell drift upstairs and invade my bedroom. Time to go face the ultimate boss monster: Dinnertime Dad, who will surely have gone berserk by now. Shields up, swords out. I bring up the game menu and click Log Out.

The screen goes black.

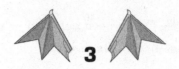

3

HANNAH

A herd of screaming toddlers is my cue: twenty minutes of sweet, sweet gaming time left.

The public library is a pretty great place to get my *Affinity* fix, all things considered. They have the fastest internet in town, which makes up for my hand-me-down laptop's painful slowness. The tables in the teen area are small, so when I put my computer and backpack on top, it leaves zero room for random people to sit with me. The librarians have known me since I was a baby, so they keep me stocked with drawing books and otherwise leave me alone. It's a pretty good deal.

I push my earbuds in deeper and turn up the volume a few notches, letting the *Affinity* background music drown out the little kids and chatty adults. The evening story time crowd is full of parents like my mom. They all work during the morning story times but manage to get to the library once per week to talk to other adults while the children's librarian entertains their kids. I used to be one of those kids.

I'm not four years old anymore, though. Now I'm thirteen.

Instead of my mom bringing me, I come straight here after school while Mom heads to her second job. Instead of dinner at home afterward, it's something off the dollar menu from the McDonald's next door.

And instead of songs and picture books, it's as many matches of *Affinity* as I can cram in before the library closes.

At six p.m.

Right when the big announcement is supposed to happen, of course.

Woe is me, I am cursed by the gamer gods. At least I can enjoy the party until then. Gotta be able to tell Tankasaurus-Rex about it tomorrow. Good tanks are hard to come by, and I want to stay on his friends list. He's almost as good as I am. I haven't told anyone, but I'm the number two melee DPS in the game. Rankings aren't public, so I have no way to check, but I'm willing to bet TRex is top ten material.

Then a private message pops up from the only person I ever really talk to, in game or IRL.

[Private Message]

Starzzle: Hey, wanna queue up for a match?

I smile—just a *little* bit—and type out a reply. Starzzle is an awesome healer who I normally love to group up with, but there's no way I'm going to miss this party.

> **PunchyTime:** Didn't you see about the
> announcement? Come to the Hub! I'm
> next to our tree.
>
> **Starzzle:** I was AFK, what did I miss?
>
> **Starzzle:** Is that a giant platypus on
> the center stage?

I swing my camera around to look, and yep, that is one *enormous* duck-billed platypus. The usual *Affinity* background music fades out and is replaced by the opening to a newish song by a band I like . . . and the platypus rears back on its hind legs to dance along.

What. Is. Even. Happening.

> **PunchyTime:** That is definitely a giant
> dancing platypus, and I have no
> idea why.
>
> **Starzzle:** Don't question it. Embrace
> the platypus. He is our master now.

I bust out laughing, then slap a hand over my mouth and glance around. Don't wanna get kicked out of the only place I have to go, but I can't help it—Starzzle's sense of humor gets me every time. I wish she went to my school, or lived in my town. She's the closest thing I have to a friend. She's hilarious, *and* she's a gamer. We hang out in game almost every night, though, which is just as good, in my opinion. I don't actually have to deal with a real live human, but I still get to have someone to talk to and game with. Win-win.

I head over to the giant purple tree in front of the Starlight Quarter, the place where we meet up every time we play together. It's taller than the buildings of the Nanotech Quarter, with bright stars dotting each branch. Can't miss it, and since Starzzle is a Star Mender, it's right near her apartment in the Starlight Quarter.

While I wait for her to show up, I swap over to the outfit I've been working on for hanging out around the Hub. I could wear the armor I use during matches, but one of the things I love about this game is how artistic you can be. My school has one terrible art class taught by a teacher who doesn't care about my *Affinity* character sketches . . . or his job in general. I'm not really good at anything else, so school is pretty much the worst. *Affinity* lets me create custom clothing and decals for my character, so I can actually do the things I'm good at.

It just so happens that I'm good at kicking people in the face, too. Virtually, I mean.

I bounce my leg under the table, make my character run in circles, and chew on the end of my messy braided brown hair while I wait. Gross, I know, but better than chewing my nails. My hands are already super pale, cracked, and bone-dry from winter. They can't take any more punishment. I can never sit still, in person *or* in the game, without my head getting all uncomfortable and buzzy. I don't have to wait long, though—

23

Starzzle literally hops onto my screen, bouncing back and forth with excitement. She's got her character dressed up in a galaxy-themed suit I designed for her, along with the rare legendary Lunar Staff that takes hours and hours of running different match types to make. It's a beautiful thing, totally worth showing off.

That's what we all do at these big in-game parties, anyway. Now is the time to pull out every rare shiny thing you have and put it on for all to see. I open up my character wardrobe and click to put on my own favorite legendary weapons, the Dark Gauntlets. These gloves took me nearly six months to earn, and I am *absolutely* going to show them off.

Starzzle: Come on, stop messing with your outfit and let's goooooo

Starzzle: I want to be up close. I heard a rumooooor

Starzzle: And if it's true, you will DEFINITELY want to have a front-row seat for the celebrity guest

PunchyTime: Okay that is not even
    slightly fair

PunchyTime: Vagueness is for losers
    and YOU MUST TELL ME

Starzzle makes her character curtsey daintily in reply, then hits her speed boost and blasts off toward the center stage, leaving a cloud of sparkling stars behind.

I will *fight* her. I will challenge her to a duel and I will CRUSH her. She can't leave me hanging like that! She knows better than anyone what I'm hoping for. Who I'm hoping to see. The excitement and frustration pops and sparks in my chest like it does right at the end of a match, when we're seconds away from winning. But what if I have to leave the library before I get to see the special guest? If it is who I think it is . . . I'm afraid to even think her name. I don't want to jinx it.

I charge after Starzzle, trailed by purple flames and a flock of tiny demons.

It's ten minutes till the announcement, and the party is in full swing. The Hub is so jammed with people that the overwhelming lights and colors almost hurt

my eyes. People shoot off old fireworks saved from the New Year's Eve event back in December. Others bounce around casting whatever spells produce the prettiest effects. Two guys in cat outfits duel with fishing poles up on the stage. A girl runs past with the Twin Blades of the Forest strapped to her back, the result of a quest chain so long, most people don't bother. Major respect. All around us, people summon tiny pet polar bears and pixies and robots that insult you when clicked on. Finally, I spot Starzzle at the edge of the stage.

PunchyTime: Okay, spill, who is this celebrity guest?

Starzzle: Nope

PunchyTime: Is it one of the developers?

Starzzle: Nope

PunchyTime: Is it a famous streamer?

Starzzle: Nope

PunchyTime: Is it your mom?

Starzzle: Nope

PunchyTime: Are you saying Nope to everything no matter what?

Starzzle: Nope

I give up. She is impossible. I type **/dance** to make my character dance along to the music, then doodle a cartoonish version of Starzzle with a giant rock bonking her on the head in the margin of my ignored social studies homework. Beside it, I draw my own character tapping her foot impatiently. This thing needs to *start*.

5:55 p.m. The teen librarian walks past, waving at me with a smile like she does every night. The wave means "Hi, Hannah, good to see you, I wish you'd come back to our Teen Advisory Group again, but also don't lose track of time, we're closing in five minutes." It's a complicated wave.

UGH. Maybe they'll make the announcement early? If I miss it, it will be *tragic*.

Then a low bass note thrums through my earbuds, the start to a fast, rhythmic beat. A bright white comet zooms on-screen from nowhere. It falls from the sky and crashes down right in the center of the stage, exploding into a blast of bright colors. When the light dies down, it reveals a giant figure with a microphone, wearing a Hurricane Games T-shirt. He towers over us all, at least twenty times bigger than a regular *Affinity* character. You could probably see him from anywhere in the entire Hub.

"Welcome, Affiniteks, to the announcement of a once-in-a-lifetime opportunity!" he says, his voice booming over the music. "My name is Mark Chowdhury, lead community manager for Hurricane Games. We've got an incredible evening planned for you. As excited as I am about the news we're sharing tonight, though, I know someone you'd much rather hear it from instead."

His character turns with a flourish, gesturing toward the sky. Above us, the stars all explode into different colors, becoming an awesome light show flashing in time to a superfast-paced song.

Yes, they *are* starting early! 5:56 p.m. . . . maybe I'll get lucky after all. Just make the announcement already! Starzzle and I chat while the music rages in the background.

PunchyTime: Oh man I am SO HYPED

PunchyTime: What do you think it'll be?

Starzzle: Is it too soon for an expansion? *Affinity* hasn't even been out for a year

PunchyTime: I HOPE IT'S AN EXPANSION

PunchyTime: With new affinities and tekniks

Starzzle: uh-oh

STARZZLE HAS GONE OFFLINE.

Poor Starzzle. One of her siblings must have walked into the room. For reasons she's never explained, Starzzle hides her gaming from her entire family, and she has a habit of randomly dropping offline when someone's about to catch her at it. She must be internally screaming over having to drop right before the announcement. The song comes to a close with a dramatic BOOM, and with a burst of rainbow sparkles, a second towering figure appears on the stage. She has bright pink hair, and deep brown skin, and splashes of rainbow glitter high on both cheeks. She looks just like she does in real life.

I let out an audible squeak and cover my mouth with both hands.

Starzzle is gonna be *so* mad.

It's Glitz. Top-paid pro girl gamer in the United States. Winner of major tournaments in *Overwatch* and *Fortnite*. Gaming influencer, top Twitch streamer, brand rep for all the best gamer gear companies. My personal hero. I want to *be* her. Starzzle idolizes her almost as hard as I do, which is part of how we got to be friends. I wish she could have stayed so we could scream about this together. Because it is definitely taking *everything* I have to not scream out loud in the middle of this library.

"Helloooo, Affiniteks!" she says, and I squeak again at the sound of her familiar voice. I've watched her videos almost as much as I've played the game myself. "Hurricane Games invited me here tonight to help them kick off an exciting new phase of the game. I love *Affinity* myself, and I could not be more thrilled about what I have to tell you tonight."

Aaaagh, so much buildup. Normally I could listen to Glitz forever, but the clock reads 5:59 p.m. Get *on* with it!

"This coming fall . . . Hurricane Games is officially launching . . ."

She pauses long enough for me to die a thousand times inside. The clock hits 6:00 p.m.

". . . a *professional* Affinity *eSports league!*"

My resulting screech is *so loud* in the silent, empty library.

"And, to celebrate," Glitz continues, "they will be hosting the first-ever *Affinity* Invitational Tournament, with livestreamed matches featuring the top players in the game! The tournament winner will receive a grand prize so amazing that it will remain secret . . . for now . . . but other prizes up for grabs include GamerTech laptops, accessories like headsets and gaming mice, and thousands of dollars in cash."

The crowd goes *nuts.* There's no voice chat in the Hub, only in matches, but if there were it would just be one giant scream. All around me, avatars jump up and down and light up the air with spells. The chat log scrolls faster than I could possibly read, filled with capital letters and exclamation points. Mark from Hurricane takes over again for the next part.

"We're beyond thrilled to have Glitz signed on as captain of our first professional US-based *Affinity* team. And, to top off our prize package, we'll be flying our winner out to Los Angeles, California, to meet Glitz in person at the LA eSports Convention!"

My brain short-circuits.

Brand-new gaming gear.

Cash.

The eSports Convention.

Meeting Glitz.

I could *meet Glitz.*

I *must* get into this tournament.

"So, you're probably wondering how you can enter the tournament, right?" the Hurricane guy says.

Obviously. All the assembled players jump around or make their characters throw their arms in the air in response.

"Well, like Glitz said, this tournament is an invitational," he continues. "Meaning, participation will be by invitation only."

My heart sinks.

Well, there goes that dream. It was nice while it lasted. There's no way they're gonna invite some thirteen-year-old kid who plays a weird class combo no one likes.

"We want to showcase the most elite-ranked players from our everyday player base. No special recruits, no outside ringers . . . just regular *Affinity* players like you. We want to show the world just how awesome an *Affinity* Pro League can be!"

Based on ranking? If it's *purely* ranking, no age limits or anything, then maybe I still have a shot. Maybe I could still–

"Hannah, closing time, pack it up, please!" the librarian says, knocking gently on my table to get my attention. I rip the earbuds out of my ears in horror, turning on my saddest, most pleading eyes.

"Please–" I start, then pause and clear my throat. I haven't talked to anyone in hours and my voice is all weird. "Please, Ms. Hayley, can I stay just two more minutes? This is really important!"

My eyes actually well up a little bit, with real shining tears and everything. This really *is* important to me. It could mean *everything*. Ms. Hayley looks over her shoulder, then nods toward the front door.

"I can't let you stay in the building," she says. "But the Wi-Fi is just strong enough to reach outside if you sit next to the window of the story-time room."

I nod, sweeping my coat off the back of my chair and shoving my arms into the sleeves as fast as I can. "Thank you. Thank you *so* much. Have a good night!"

I throw my bag over my shoulder, pick up my laptop with it still open and running the game, and stick one earbud back in my ear as I walk-run toward the front door. Hurricane Games Mark is still talking.

". . . eligible to participate. If you have any questions, we'll be posting all the details to our website first thing in the morning."

No, I missed the exact part I needed to hear! Am I eligible or not? Will being thirteen keep me out?

As soon as I step outside, the cold bites at my exposed fingers. February is the *worst*. I press myself up against the freezing window of the story room just like Ms. Hayley told me to, trying not to look like too much of a creeper. The game lags and stutters, the sound breaking up, and I look on in horror as the Wi-Fi signal ticks down to three bars, then two. The movements of the other characters around me go all jagged, and the visual effects start to glitch out. No, no, no, please!

"S-s-s-sooo-o, keep an–on your–box to see i-i-if you've been–"

I growl in sheer frustration, pressing so close to the window I'll probably leave an imprint of my face behind. What is he saying? We'll get a message if we're chosen? Like an email, or like an in-game message? When will they get sent? When will I *know*?

Then my in-game mail pings with a cheerful chime.

YOU HAVE 1 NEW MESSAGE.

. . . No.

There's *no way.* It's too soon, right? It has to be too soon.

With shaking fingers, I open my inbox. There's a single unread message at the top of the list.

It's from Hurricane Games.

Oh.

My.

GOD.

LARKIN

The computer/dog/plant room at the back of our house is an obnoxiously busy place to be a secret gamer. My brother's constant last-minute homework panic. My sister's burning need to roll on the floor with the dogs at random times. My parents wandering in to shuffle through the endless stacks of papers and envelopes on the computer desk. How is a girl supposed to get her precious gaming time in with all these interruptions?

Well, the early bird gets the keyboard, or something.

I crack open the door to the bedroom I share with my younger sister and look left, then right. The coast is clear. I walk slowly down the hall, totally calm. Nothing to see here. Just walking, already dressed for school in a skirt with lime-green tights and boots. My short blue-streaked hair is in a perfect spiky mess, clipped back from my pale face. Totally ready to go. No reason to stop me for nagging purposes.

My sister's terrible off-key singing is only partially drowned out by the shower. My older brother is already in the kitchen, scarfing oatmeal before the bus for high school comes, if the spoon-on-bowl clinking is anything to go by. My parents are nowhere to be seen–probably out feeding the animals and tending to the huge tables full of seedlings in the garage. This is my best chance.

I love it when I can get an *Affinity* match in before school. This early in the morning, the matches are really chill warm-ups for the day. I get my fingers going and get strategies brewing in my head. That way, when I get home from band practice after school, I'm already primed for some serious-ranked matches.

It's also the easiest time to slip in here unnoticed. Just me and the dogs, who are taking their post-breakfast, pre-squirrel-chasing nap on their beds along the back wall. One side wall is almost all windows, and the long table there is filled with little potted plants grown by me and my sister. Tiny cacti, succulents, herbs, and a huge vine of cucumbers crawling up a rack with a warm light above it.

And against the other wall is a desk with our shared family computer. On that computer, inside a folder called Larkin's School Stuff, is the icon to launch *Affinity*.

I double-click it and spin impatiently in the desk chair while it loads. A screen with the *Affinity* logo pops up, and the dramatic opening music plays through the computer speakers at full volume. I scramble for my headset and plug it in, then freeze. Did anyone hear?

The shower runs in the background. One of the dogs kicks the other in his sleep. An annoyed grumble follows.

Silence.

Safe, I think. The game loads up with my character right where I logged out last night, in the Hub next to center stage. I scowl. I can't believe my little sister stormed in here last night right before the big announcement. She ended up hogging the computer until the "no screens o'clock" deadline my parents monitor like hawks, so I never even got to read one of the news sites to see what it was. I was really looking forward to playing a few matches afterward, too.

But as soon as I log in, my private messages blow up.

[Private Message]

PunchyTime: YOU'RE HERE

PunchyTime: oh man you are going to FLIP OUT

PunchyTime: You would not believe what the announcement was

PunchyTime: AND THE SPECIAL GUEST LSKAJHLFHKLASDJFHS

PunchyTime: and I have NEWS

I look at the clock, confused. It's definitely morning, right? Before school on a Tuesday? And Punchy is online?

> **Starzzle:** How are you here? I thought you didn't have internet at home.
>
> **PunchyTime:** I do, it's just so slow I can't even upload my homework on it. The game barely runs and I keep getting kicked offline.

As if to prove her point, she drops offline without warning. Such cruelty. How can she get me hyped like that and disappear? I hate her internet with the passion of a thousand toxic gamer babies. The little envelope icon for my in-game messages has a red circle with a (1) on it, so I click it to pass the time until Punchy gets back.

Dear Starzzle,

CONGRATULATIONS from the team at Hurricane Games!

This is your official invitation to participate in the *Affinity* Pro League Launch Invitational Tournament in the role of healer. You're receiving this invitation because you rank among the top 64 players of your role in the United States, and we're excited for you to show off your skills to the entire country in honor of our upcoming professional eSports league.

Within 24 hours, you will receive an email at your registered email address with all the details about the tournament, including the link to a private forum where 64 teams will be formed. Each player will post an introduction, after which you will be free to group up into your own teams of four, with one person in each role. We can also randomly assign you to a team, if you prefer. Your team will have one month to train together before the tournament begins.

There's more, but my brain stops right there.

Um. What?

WHAT??

I quickly google the name of the tournament and turn up a huge list of articles on every major gaming news site with the details of the tournament. And the prizes.

And the special celebrity guest who announced it. Who I can meet if I win. The rumors were true.

I'm going to feed my sister's entire collection of horse figurines to the goats. They are her ultimate treasure, and the punishment must be severe for making me miss out on Glitz.

I Alt+Tab back over to *Affinity* and find that Punchy's back, and she's sent me a giant string of messages I can't possibly keep up with. But the one right at the bottom is all I really need to know.

PunchyTime: I GOT INVITED TO PLAY IN THE TOURNAMENT. I AM DYING WITH AWESOMENESS.

I grin so hard, my cheeks hurt. My fingers pound against the keys with the force of my excitement.

Starzzle: PUNCHY

Starzzle: PUNCHY

Starzzle: PUNCHY

Starzzle: I GOT INVITED TOO

Starzzle: We are going to wreck SO MANY FACES

PunchyTime: So. Many. Faces.

PunchyTime: Hold on, my tank friend got in, too. Let me make us a group chat.

TANKASAURUSREX HAS JOINED THE CHAT CHANNEL.

PunchyTime: TRex, this is Starzzle, my amazing healer friend who will also be in the tournament!

PunchyTime: Star, this is the tank I grouped with yesterday that I told you about.

Starzzle: Nice name, Tankasaurus

TankasaurusRex: Thanks. Grats on getting into the tournament

PunchyTime: So look, I know there are 253 other players who got chosen, and we're supposed to meet everyone on the forums

Dang right I do. As soon as I signed up for the game, I looked up the most popular healer builds and deliberately chose the one nobody plays. Why should I play like everyone else? I check TRex's character profile. I don't think I've ever healed a Rune Knight in a match before. And I've definitely never run with another Demon Puncher. Punchy is one of a kind.

Starzzle: HEY.

PunchyTime: <3 <3 <3

TankasaurusRex: Yeah, I don't know though.

TankasaurusRex: The parent permission slip might not go so well. I'm not sure I'll be able to play in the tournament.

TankasaurusRex: I'm going to try, though. I have to at least ask.

Wait, what? Permission slip?

I bring the message back up and actually read the whole thing this time, including the bit at the bottom that I missed. Sure enough, the last paragraph has the potential to be a serious life-ruiner. Because there's one major thing–besides lacking my own computer–that could destroy my chances of playing in this tournament.

All participants under the age of 18 will need to submit a permission form signed by a parent or legal guardian in order to take part in the tournament. The form is due by the end of the week, at which point your spot in the tournament

will be forfeited. The form and further details will be
included in the email to follow.

Again, congratulations from all of us at
Hurricane Games!

I let my head fall and bang my forehead against the desk.
A parent permission slip. Of all things.

My heart rolls over and dies in my chest.

I haven't told *anyone* IRL that I play *Affinity*.

My friends at school don't know. I'm first-chair clarinet in
all-district band, and my band friends all want me to group
up with them for Solo and Ensemble competition. I got cast
for the spring play, and my theater friends want me to run
lines with them after school. And my parents . . . they would
never understand. They're hippie homesteaders who grow
food and make homemade jam and bake bread and raise
chickens. They're also totally focused on my brother and me
getting into a good college, even though I'm only in middle
school.

And most important, they *hate* video games. My brother
failed ninth grade and had to repeat it because he got ad-
dicted to a game, so they banned all video gaming from our
house. They would probably lay eggs themselves if they
knew how much I played.

Everyone wants me to do whatever *they* think is most important. Of all the things I do, gaming is the one thing every

person in my life would agree should be at the bottom of the list. Or not on the list at all.

But what I want—more than *anything*—is to be a professional gamer.

It's a dream so secret I've only ever told Punchy, and only because she loves Glitz as much as I do. We've been talking about livestreaming *Affinity* together as soon as I turn thirteen, the age limit for creating our own channel. This tournament would be a big step toward my dream. If I got that prize money, it would show everyone that being a pro gamer is a real thing, and a thing I could do. Because I'm good. I know I am.

I really could win this.

PunchyTime: Hey, I gotta go to school

PunchyTime: But since we're going to be gaming together all the time for the next month, you can call me by my real name

PunchyTime: I'm Hannah.

TankasaurusRex: I'm Josh. Thanks for the invite.

I hesitate.

It's a weird line to cross. This will be the first time I connect anything gaming-related with my real name. To other real humans. The first time I really own this thing I love so much with my real-life self. My fingers hover over the keyboard.

Starzzle: I'm Larkin. Nice to meet y'all.

Pro gaming world, here I come.

5

WHEATLEY

TEAM ASSIGNMENT

TEAM NAME:

The Weird Ones

EXISTING PLAYERS:

TANKASAURUSREX: (Tank—Rune Knight—Runes + Sword Knight)
PUNCHYTIME: (Melee DPS—Demon Puncher— Demonology + Martial Artist)
STARZZLE: (Healer—Star Mender—Starlight + Mender)

I don't know how I'm supposed to barge into a group of three people who already know each other. So many other teams had only two people who chose to group up, and a couple teams were entirely random assignments.

Either of those situations would be easier than this. Being the rando shoved into a group of friends would be difficult for anyone, even someone without my secrets.

FACT: People don't like outsiders.

FACT: They wouldn't like me if they knew me for real.

CONCLUSION?

Be someone else.

That's the beauty of online interaction: I can be who I want to be instead of who I am. What makes a person like-able? What kind of person does this team need?

I go back to their introduction posts on the forum and reread them to look for clues.

NOTES

TANKASAURUSREX/JOSH: kind, loyal, serious, shy

PUNCHYTIME/HANNAH: prickly, determined, clever, sarcastic

STARZZLE/LARKIN: enthusiastic, creative, expressive, dedicated

TEAM: All play strange, unpopular class combos. All are 12–13 years old. All are very serious about winning this tournament.

Well, maybe I'll fit better than I thought. I'm young, too, I guess. I definitely want to do a good job in this tournament. And my weird class combo is a literal perfect fit, designed for this exact team. I'm a Nano Ranger, a ranged DPS class combo that wields swarms of tiny nanorobots. It's really rare because it's difficult to be any good at it. I know I'm a good player. That's not my problem.

I have some other skills of my own to bring, too. I'm very good with computers. I know the technical side of the game inside and out. When it comes to working with other people, though, practicing for hours, getting to know them, letting them get to know me . . .

I have to make them like me if we're going to have any hope of winning. Can I be funny? Everyone likes someone who's funny. Let me search for my sense of humor . . .

ERROR: FILE NOT FOUND.

Ha ha ha. Being funny is hard. Maybe I can learn?

But then I get a message from my "dad," or the closest thing I have to one.

> You're stalling.

I wish he could see me scowl.

> I'm strategizing.

I don't know why I bother to talk back, though.

> Just get logged in and talk
> to your team already,

Logically, I know he's right, but I still can't stop the unpleasant *something* bouncing around in my brain. I brace myself to meet my new team and launch the game before I can question myself even more. It's storming right now. Maybe the internet will go out and buy me some time.

The game loads way too quickly, of course. My system is lightning fast.

Lightning fast. And there's lightning outside. Ha ha? Is that funny?

. . . I'm gonna guess no.

My character loads up in the last place I logged him out, in the Nanotech Quarter of the Hub. I took forever designing him at character creation–lime-green hair spilling out from under his hood, glowing wires running under his skin from just below his ears down to his shoulders, and lightweight jet-black armor that lets me fade right into the shadows. Playing this character is the only time I get to have any control over how I look, so I'm constantly tweaking things and hunting down rare modifications. I'm one achievement away from getting a new mod for my bow, so I go to queue up for a match . . . then catch a flurry of activity in my chat log.

People are talking to me.

JOINED CHAT CHANNEL THE WEIRD ONES.

You have been added to this channel by a GM and cannot leave without GM permission. Any team disputes should be taken up with the tournament master.

Starzzle: HE'S HERE

Starzzle: Okay everyone, be cool

Starzzle: Hello and welcome to team weirdos! We're so glad you're here!

PunchyTime: Don't scare him, Lark

PunchyTime: Uh, hi, I guess?

PunchyTime: Sending a summon

A message box pops up with a cheerful sound effect:

PUNCHYTIME WOULD LIKE TO SUMMON YOU TO THEIR LOCATION. ACCEPT?

YES   NO

Starzzle: Come join us in our shiny new team hall!

I hit YES before I have a chance to freeze up with doubt. It's fine. I can do this. This is what I'm here for. There's a quick loading screen, then I emerge into an area I've never seen before. It's a huge open space filled with training dummies and furniture, with floor-to-ceiling windows that show the Hub far below. We're floating above the city! I've never bothered with player apartments before. Never had anyone to visit me, and I didn't need the extra storage space, so why bother?

Now I get it. *Everything* is customizable. We can make a team logo to paint on the floor of the training ring. We can get different furniture and add weird trinkets and robots and lights and animals and . . . This is like character creation times nine thousand. I want *all of it*.

Then a guy in gleaming silver armor steps directly in front of me and waves.

> **TankasaurusRex**: Good to have you on the team. Love the class combo.

Oh, right, there are people here. Do the people thing now, spend hours customizing our team hall later.

This is my chance. First impression. Don't mess it up.

I type /**wave** to make my character wave back, then say my first ever words to my new team. . . .

> **EatUrWheaties:** Thanks, who doesn't love deadly swarms of bees?

. . . I am already *the worst* at this.

> **EatUrWheaties:** I mean, like nano robotic bees
> **EatUrWheaties:** Because I have an ability called Electric Swarm that
> **EatUrWheaties:** Never mind
> **EatUrWheaties:** Hi, nice to meet you

Well, that's it. I've blown it.

A girl in a purple sparkly suit sails across my screen from left to right, then jumps back across from right to left, over and over. A trail of glittering stars follows her every move. Probably the enchantment on the Lunar Staff strapped to her back. Somehow she manages to type out a response while in constant motion:

> **Starzzle:** Omg I love him already
> **TankasaurusRex:** I think we'll get along just fine

Huh. Okay. Stunningly, they don't hate me yet. There's still one person left, though. I turn to look at the last member of the team, Hannah, who is in the process of utterly destroying a target dummy. Her character leaps into close range, unleashes a flurry of jabs, then sprouts glowing demon wings as she flips over the dummy's shoulder and kicks its head clean off. The head rolls across the floor and stops near my feet, smiling up at me. Her foe vanquished, Hannah turns to me and pumps a fist in the air.

PunchyTime: I would definitely like to see some noobs get swarmed by angry robo-bees

PunchyTime: So let's go wreck some faces, now that we have our full team together!

Starzzle: YES

In an excited flurry, Starzzle jumps circles around Josh, who simply stands there and takes it.

TankasaurusRex: Yeah, I can do one more before dinner

PunchyTime: Are you having The Permission Slip Convo tonight?

TankasaurusRex: Yep. Wish me all the
    luck.

TankasaurusRex: ALL of it. I'll need
    it.

Starzzle: Save some for me. I'm doing
    the same tonight.

PunchyTime: Good luck, both. My mom
    didn't even look at the paper
    before she signed it. I'm g2g.

PunchyTime: What about you, Wheat?

Hah.

EatUrWheaties: Yeah, not a problem for
    me

EatUrWheaties: my dad WANTS me in the
    tournament

As close to the truth as I can get.

EatUrWheaties: Anyway, yes, faces.

EatUrWheaties: Let's wreck some.

EatUrWheaties: My bees are hungry

My bees are hungry? Of all the words in the English language, those are the ones I chose?

> **TankasaurusRex**: So your bees don't
> eat honey like regular bees?

Okay, another opportunity. Stick the landing this time, Wheatley.

> **EatUrWheaties**: Absolutely not. They feast
> only on the souls of my enemies.

Nope, nope, too intense, dial it back. How to make it less creepy?

> **EatUrWheaties**: :)

NO, that's *worse*, what am I *doing*? Achievement unlocked: Maximum creepiness.

> **Starzzle**: BAHAHAHAHA

Starzzle: Amazing

PunchyTime: They will see the name
The Weird Ones and tremble before
us. And the bees.

TankasaurusRex: 100% yes. Ready to
queue up for a match?

PunchyTime: FINALLY

Starzzle: YES do iiiiiiit

Oh. I guess we're playing our first match together *right now*. No pressure. Everything is *fine*.

EatUrWheaties: Ready to go!

. . . I guess.

Just before the match loads up, though, a string of private messages pops up:

[Private Message]

Starzzle: Hey, I just wanted to say
welcome to you and your bees again

Starzzle: We're really excited you're here!

Starzzle: Thanks for joining us

Wow.

I guess . . . maybe this won't be so hard after all?

> **EatUrWheaties**: Thanks, Star. It's nice
> of you all to take me in. Glad to
> be here.
>
> **Starzzle**: You can call me Larkin:)

Then the notice pops up with a burst of dramatic music:

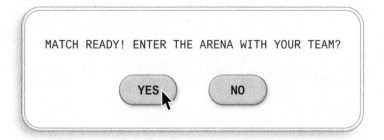

> MATCH READY! ENTER THE ARENA WITH YOUR TEAM?
>
> YES   NO

Ready or not . . .

I choose yes.

JOSH

Well, this is a total disaster.

Hurricane Games has apparently decided that everyone playing in the tournament should get a special flag next to the name over their head, so *everyone* in the game can know exactly who they're up against. And maybe in some cases that would be a good thing. Intimidation factor, or a little less trash talk.

In this match? It may as well be a giant target on our foreheads. These people we're fighting can't wait to earn the bragging rights that come with utterly destroying a tournament team in 4v4 free-for-all, and they are *not* shy about telling us.

> **Natzgo:** How did such a **HECKIN GOOD DOGGO** get a tournament invite?
> **cakelegend:** his daddy probably works for hurricane

I actually laugh out loud at that. The idea of my dad having *anything* to do with video games is hilarious. He would need a two-hour tutorial on how to make his character run with the WASD keys. It's much more likely to be my mom who'd work for Hurricane. She's the one who's actually a programmer, and so good at what she does that she keeps getting promoted and making us move. I'd love it if she'd be a little *less* good, actually. I'm getting really tired of eating lunch alone at school.

And for once, the chat filter is a fail. Not sure I love being called a doggo, even if I am a heckin' good one.

I slip out from behind the crumbling building that's been providing me with cover and start making my way across the middle of the map. Larkin should be respawning any second, and I need to be there to protect her when she does. I swing my camera around, left, right, and behind. Nothing.

Then the other team's Green Rogue drops out of stealth and stuns me. In three seconds flat, I'm dazed, dying of three different poisons, and being choked by vines. Maybe I'm a heckin' *bad* doggo after all.

I hate Green Rogues. They're the most basic, common, *obnoxious* class combo in the game. Nature plus stabby Rogue-type character might not seem like an obvious combination, but those poisons are game-breakingly powerful. If a Green

Rogue manages to stun you, that's it–you're almost guaran-
teed to die horribly.

Like me. I am dying horribly, right here, right now. Case
in point: my character falls on top of his shield, surrounded
by a puddle of green goo and limp vines. Dead again. I lean
back in my chair and rub my hands over my face with a
frustrated groan. The only way to keep a Green Rogue from
wrecking a whole team is to have a really great ranged DPS
ready to pick them off from far away. Or maybe a healer with
quick reflexes to dispel the stun.

We're *supposed* to have both of those on this team.

TankasaurusRex: Wheat, where are you??

TankasaurusRex: Star??

With nothing to do until the respawn counter brings me back to life, I swing my camera around to study the battle happening above my corpse. Hannah is pummeling my attacker and winning, but there's another player sneaking up on her. That won't end well. I sigh. This match is hot garbage.

I skim over the combat log to see if I can figure out what's going on.

STARZZLE HAS GONE OFFLINE.

STARZZLE HAS COME ONLINE.

STARZZLE HAS GONE OFFLINE.

EATURWHEATIES HAS BEEN ELIMINATED.

EatUrWheaties: wwwwwwwwwwwwwwwwwww

EATURWHEATIES HAS BEEN ELIMINATED.

EatUrWheaties: wwwwwwwwwwwwww

EATURWHEATIES HAS BEEN ELIMINATED.

STARZZLE HAS COME ONLINE.

> **PunchyTime:** W, what is going on? You
>   were running into that wall for
>   like a minute straight
> **PunchyTime:** STAR I SWEAR
>
>   STARZZLE HAS GONE OFFLINE.
>
> **EatUrWheaties:** wwwwwwwwwwwwwwwww
>   wwwwwwwwwwwwwwwwwwwwwwwwww
> **PunchyTime:** UGH, I guess I'll just DO
>   THIS MYSELF

In the last few seconds before I disappear from my pile of poison and shame on the floor, I see Hannah's character go sailing overhead, boosted by glowing purple demon wings. She lands in between the Rogue and the teammate that snuck up on her, a Rune Sorcerer, and unleashes all her fury. She blows every single major cooldown she has and puts up an incredible fight that makes me grateful she's on *our* team. Two against one, though, and two of the most unbalanced, overpowered class combos in the game? She doesn't stand a chance. She crumples to the ground just as I reappear back at the spawn point, fuming. I squeeze the mouse so hard that it gives an ominous creaking sound, then force myself to let go and shake out the tension in my hands.

What is *happening*? Why are we so bad? I really thought we'd be better than this. We're all good players on our own, but as a team, we're *terrible.* If we keep playing like this, we'll get laughed out of the first round of the tournament and probably never speak to each other again, and my parents will think they were right about my gaming all along.

I blow out a slow breath. Don't panic. Chill. Think.

Okay, someone has to try to organize this mess. Probably no one will listen to me, or they'll get mad at me or something. But I have to try.

[Team Chat]

TankasaurusRex: Okay, let's regroup. Everyone meet at the River of Light and we'll take them on together.

EatUrWheaties: wwwwwwwwwwwwwwwww

[Match Chat]

cakelegend: hahahaha, how many times do you think I can kill this FLUFFY ranger guy?

EATURWHEATIES HAS BEEN ELIMINATED.

EATURWHEATIES HAS BEEN ELIMINATED.

EATURWHEATIES HAS BEEN ELIMINATED.

This might actually be the worst match I've ever played. I don't know if it's even salvageable at this point.

At my feet, Marvin the Dog grumbles and farts. I sigh.

Agreed, Marvin.

Totally agreed.

[Team Chat]

PunchyTime: You know what? Forget you all

I groan and type as fast as I can, trying to intercept her.

TankasaurusRex: Hannah, CHILL, just wait for me and we can

She dives straight back in before I can finish typing.

She falls to the ground barely thirty seconds later.

. . . never mind.

The match ends quickly from there. In a team-based free-for-all, it's first team to thirty eliminations or whoever has the most eliminations before the ten-minute timer runs out.

We barely last five minutes.

BLUE TEAM: DEFEAT!

Totally destroyed.

Marvin gets up and wanders away, apparently embarrassed to be seen with me. Honestly, I don't blame him.

We all reappear at our team hall after the match ends, standing awkwardly in the middle of the room. Except for Wheatley, who is running into a wall. Larkin must have logged back in at some point, because she's with us. Her normally jumping, running, dancing avatar is totally still. I fold my arms on the desk and lay my head down.

Okay, morale is clearly low. Understandable, after a solid fail like that. I'm feeling pretty awful, too. But if we're going to have any hope of getting past the first round of the tournament, we can't let this get us down. We're off to a rough start, but we can turn it around. I wait around for another few seconds to see if someone else will start making the inspiring speech . . . but no one does.

Guess that means it falls to me? Ugh. I'm no good at this.

[Team Chat]

TankasaurusRex: Hey, look, it's okay. This was just one match. Our first one. We just have to figure out how to work together.

TankasaurusRex: We play weird class combos. That's our whole thing.

> **TankasaurusRex:** So it'll just take a bit longer to figure out how to play off each other than it would normally
>
> **EatUrWheaties:** wwwwwwwwwwwwwwwwwwww wwwwwwwwwwwwwwwwwwwwwwwwwwwwwww

There's a long, awkward silence.

> **Starzzle:** It's nice of you to say so, Josh
>
> **Starzzle:** But I'm pretty sure we're doomed
>
> **PunchyTime:** Yeah, this is going to be a horrific dumpster fire
>
> **PunchyTime:** Especially if, no offense, you can't STOP DROPPING OFFLINE, LARK
>
> **PunchyTime:** It drove me nuts before, but now that the tournament is on the line?
>
> **PunchyTime:** You have to cut it out

Ouch. A bit harsh, but . . . true.

> **TankasaurusRex:** I don't want to be
> a jerk, but I agree. Is it your
> internet connection?
>
> STARZZLE HAS GONE OFFLINE.

My stomach clenches. Was I too mean? I didn't want to make her mad. Now I feel awful. I really like Larkin, and I don't want this group to fall apart when we're just getting to know each other.

> **TankasaurusRex:** Were we too hard on
> her?
> **PunchyTime:** Nah, she seriously does
> this all the time. Her family
> doesn't know that she's a gamer, so
> she Alt+F4's out every time someone
> walks into the room.
> **PunchyTime:** If she weren't the best
> healer I've ever played with, I
> would never have suggested we team
> up with her.
> **PunchyTime:** I just thought she would
> like . . . stop
> **PunchyTime:** because of the
> tournament.

I look over at the permission slip sitting on the end of my desk, still unsigned. I get it, actually.

> **TankasaurusRex:** Well, her parents
>   have to sign the permission slip,
>   so they'll find out soon. Hopefully
>   that will fix it.
>
> **TankasaurusRex:** I should go, actually.
>   I need to try to get my parents
>   to sign the form tonight, and if
>   I wait too long, they'll get tired
>   and cranky and say no just so they
>   don't have to talk about it.
>
> **PunchyTime:** Good luck.
>
> **TankasaurusRex:** Thanks. Wheatley, I
>   dunno what's going on, but I'll see
>   you later, I guess.
>
> **EatUrWheaties:** wwwwwwwwwwwwwwwwwwww
>   wwwwwwwwwwwwwwwwwwwwwwwwwwwwwwwwwww
>
> **TankasaurusRex:** . . . right

I log out and slump back in my chair.

Have I picked the wrong team? Is there even any point in getting in this fight with my parents if we have no chance of making it past the first round?

I pull a notebook out of my backpack and flip through

the pages until I find the speech I wrote to try to convince them to sign the form. It's my fourth draft, and it's *still* full of red-inked corrections. I don't even write this many drafts of papers for English class. If I go in without a plan, though, I know I'll just get mad and end up ruining everything. I still want to try. I thought about lying, about giving them just the last page with the signature line and telling them it was for school, but gave up that idea fast. My parents are expert lie-catchers. Besides, what would I do if we actually won and I got a bunch of prize money and computer stuff in the mail out of nowhere? I clear my throat and start reading to warm up.

"Mom. Dad. I have a form I need signed. I know you don't really approve of my gaming, but this is really important to me. I'm really good at this game, and I got invited to a tournament and. . . . yeah, this is never going to work."

I sigh and *thunk* my head down on my keyboard, rolling it back and forth over the keys. My computer makes annoyed noises in protest, but I don't care. I just . . . I really want this. I actually, *really* care about this. And the idea of walking up to my parents and having them tell me it's stupid to care so much about a video game . . .

They have no idea. They already had coworkers, and even friends, when we moved here. As terrible as we are as a team right now, my teammates are the closest thing I have to friends at the moment, and it's really nice to have someone to talk to other than my parents. That's kinda sad, probably. But it's the truth.

I can't let them down. I have to do this.

I grab the form off my desk and throw open my bedroom door before I can change my mind. Down the stairs, follow the scent to the kitchen, and . . .

"Oh, Josh, good timing," my dad says from his place hovering over the stove. "Dinner is just about ready. Have a seat."

I mumble something in return and slide into my assigned seat, hiding the paper under my leg. How exactly do I do this? I can't just . . . randomly bring it up out of nowhere. My mom slides into the chair next to mine and lays her phone facedown on the table.

"What were you doing all evening?" she asks. "I haven't heard a peep out of you. Do you have a lot of homework?"

And there it is. The perfect opening. I take a slow breath in through my nose and try to get calm and focused, like I do right before a match starts. I'm the tank. I have to be brave, have to charge in and take the lead. The other players, their whole goal is to not get hit. It's my job to take the hits. It's my job to step right up to the scary thing and do my best to not just survive it, but to protect others.

Whether we have any hope of winning or not, my teammates are counting on me.

Here goes.

"No, I did all my homework at school, during lunch and on the bus. I was . . . playing *Affinity*, actually. With my team."

"Ugh, that game," my dad says from his place at the stove. My mom, though, looks briefly interested.

"Your team? What team is this?"

It's like she's setting me up for the perfect shot. Thanks, Mom.

"I actually wanted to talk to you about that. I actually . . ."

I actually need to stop saying the word *actually*.

Breathe. Start again.

"Hurricane Games—that's the company that makes *Affinity*—they're having a tournament to kick off their professional eSports league. It's an invitation-only tournament, so only the top sixteen players in each role got invited."

A little surge of pride boosts my confidence. The words start coming faster as more of my excitement comes out.

"I got invited. I'm number six in the country for tanking. That's like, protecting my teammates from getting hurt. I'm really good, and the tournament has some great prizes. Money, a lot of it, and free computers and stuff. I'm teamed up with three other kids my age, and we're . . ."

I don't know how true this is. But I want it to be true, so I say it anyway.

"We're actually pretty good friends. It's been nice having people to hang out with."

I look up from my hands to see my parents both watching me, the air heavy with their silence. The form crinkles as I clutch it tight, wrinkling the paper and probably smearing the ink with my sweaty hands.

Moment of truth.

I hold out the form and hope.

7

LARKIN

The folded-up permission slip in my pocket makes me feel like I'm walking around with a pocket full of lobsters. It would be impossible to forget you had wiggling, spiny-legged, giant clawed creatures trying to escape your pants, right? Everywhere you went, you'd be wondering: Can people see the lobsters? Have the lobsters escaped? You wouldn't be able to think about anything *but* lobsters.

I haven't been able to forget the form ever since I printed it out in the school library at lunch. Everywhere I went, I thought about it. Science class. Band practice. Play rehearsal after school. On the late bus home. Everywhere I went, I was sure people could see my pants lobsters and were planning to spring questions on me at any second.

Okay, the lobster thing makes less sense than I thought, but still. The feeling is accurate.

Here, sitting at the dinner table, it's impossible for anyone to see the folded-up form inside my pocket, covered by my jacket, under the dinner table, without some serious X-ray vision. And yet, I am absolutely certain this lobster is going to crawl onto the table and start dancing when I least expect it. Boom, secret out.

In some ways, maybe that would be easier.

With my sister and brother arguing over some YouTube video, my parents trying to rein them in, and the dogs surfing for scraps under the table, it's easy for me to sit quiet and unnoticed. I shovel some roasted sweet potatoes into my mouth and consider my angle of attack. I should have asked Josh what he planned to say to his parents. He seems so smart and leaderly, like his parents would take him seriously. I don't have the slightest clue how to convince my parents, whose eldest child actually failed a grade in high school because of video games, that this tournament is worthwhile. I stick my hand in my pocket and feel the edges of the folded paper. Maybe I should just hand it to them. It's pretty self-explanatory.

"Right, Lark?" my brother asks.

My head whips up, and I yank my hand out of my pocket so fast that the folded-up paper flops out onto the floor. I squeak in horror and quickly knock my napkin off my lap to cover it up.

"Um, right?" I say, hoping desperately I didn't just agree to muck out the chicken coop or give up computer time for a week or something. He's been known to do stuff like that.

My mom frowns. "Are you okay, chickadee? You seem awfully distracted."

I swallow nervously, then scoop my napkin up off the

floor with the folded-up form tucked inside. "I'm fine. Everything's fine. How are you?"

"Fine," my dad says, drawing the word out skeptically. "Did your solo go okay in band today?"

"It was fine," I answer dutifully.

"Jayla's dad called and said she asked you to be part of her quartet for Solo and Ensemble competition, but you hadn't said yes yet. Is everything okay with you and her?"

"We're fine," I answer again. I desperately need to find a word other than *fine*, but my brain has shorted out.

"What about play rehearsal?" Mom cuts in. "Are you doing well with your lines? Do you need someone to practice with? I know Sam would–"

"It was fine, Mom. Everything is fine. Band, drama, classes, my friends, my plants, it's all fine."

The awkward silence at the table descends like an alien spaceship. My parents look at each other for a parental telepathy moment.

"And there's . . . nothing you want to talk to us about?" my dad ventures, hesitant.

I do not breathe. I do not move.

This is the perfect opening. In my lap, I crush my napkin with its hidden form between both hands. Mouth, I command you to open! Say words! Tell them! *Mom, Dad, I'm a secret gamer and I need you to sign this form because I'm awesome at it and I know you won't think it's as important as band or drama or school but I really love it and I want to go pro and I know the chances of that happening are like getting bitten by a shark who's being struck by lightning but . . .*

I shake my head, mouth pressed shut, just in case the word *fine* tries to crawl its way up my throat again. Or, you know, any of the other eight million words crowding my brain right now. I don't think I can do this. They'll be so disappointed. They'll take away *Affinity*. They'll ban me from the computer and put me on extra goat duty.

I shake my head again.

"Okay," my mom says, as if she's letting it go. She is most definitely not letting it go. This conversation will rear its head again when I'm least expecting it.

"May I be excused?" I squeak out.

My dad nods. Thankfully, no one asks me why I take my napkin with me when I leave.

I run straight for the computer room while everyone's still distracted with dinner, unfolding the form as I go. The chair creaks as I flop down into it, and I smooth the paper out on the desk next to our scanner. Creases breaking up the ink. My name written into the blank in the first line. An empty signature space, with "parent/guardian signature (if player is a minor)" printed below. I skim over the form one last time, though I've read it probably twenty times already. Most of it is made up of complicated official-sounding language, but there are a few things I recognize: permission to use my first name and a submitted photo in tournament-related stuff online. That's no worse than social media. Better, actually. My parents won't mind, right?

I take a deep breath, listen for anyone coming down the hallway . . . then I grab a pen.

I sign my dad's signature on the line and slap the form on the scanner glass before I can think too hard about it. A few clicks later, and the form is scanned, attached to an email, and sent off to Hurricane Games headquarters.

A box pops up in the lower left corner for a few seconds, offering me the chance to stop the email from going through. I hold my breath . . . and the box disappears.

My racing heart begins to slow, even as my stomach twists in an uncomfortable knot.

It's done. I grab the form off the scanner and fold it up again, cramming it into that teeny-tiny useless pocket that every pair of jeans has but no one knows what to do with. It can't possibly fall out of such a tight pocket and incriminate me. I'll recycle it at school tomorrow where there's no danger of a nosy sister rooting through the office bin.

The clock ticks over to 6:30 p.m., and there's still no sign of anyone in the hallway, so I launch *Affinity,* drumming out a nervous rhythm on my leg as the game loads. Thankfully I won't have to look anyone in the face or talk to them with my actual voice. I'm a *terrible* liar.

As soon as I see my character's purple pixie hairstyle and the Lunar Staff I worked so hard to get, something inside me relaxes. At my fingertips, Starzzle spins in a circle and jumps wildly around the room, trailing glitter and magic. I click my teleportation crystal and phase into our team hall, where Hannah joins me in my restless bouncing without either of us ever saying a word. It's like when a teacher says something accidentally funny in class and you lock eyes with a friend across the room. No words necessary, just that instant click of *we both get it.*

This is where I belong. This is where I feel on solid ground. No one else makes demands of my time here. Extra ensembles, extra rehearsals, homework help, volunteering . . . I like doing all of it. Really. But here, the only ones asking me to do anything are the friends I want to be playing with anyway. *Affinity* is for *me.*

I've logged in to the middle of a conversation, apparently. One that makes me want to log right back out again.

[Team Chat]

EatUrWheaties: Did your parents sign the form, Josh?

PunchyTime: Yeah, how did it go??

TankasaurusRex: It was . . . not great. My dad yelled a lot.

TankasaurusRex: They told me it was a waste of time and you all don't count as real friends, etc. etc.

TankasaurusRex: But they signed the form, so I'm gonna call it a win

---

Lucky him. I try not to feel too bitter about it. I'm glad he gets to keep playing with us, and that's the truth. But I know what's coming next. I start typing a message to head it off:

Wanna do a practice run? We should try that obstacle course scenario that

But Hannah beats me to it before I can finish the thought.

> **PunchyTime:** How about you, Larkin? Did your parents take it okay? Are you officially out as a gamer to them?

I briefly consider telling them the truth.
But only briefly.

> **Starzzle:** Yep, good to go
> **Starzzle:** So let's practice!

I queue us up for a random training scenario without asking the team their preference, desperate to move us on from this topic and get to work. Who knows how much time I'll have before someone walks into the room and I have to log out. Again. If we're gonna have any hope of winning this tournament, I need to make use of every single second.

[Private Message]

PunchyTime: Is everything okay, Star?

And what else can I really say?

Starzzle: Yep. Everything's fine.

Just . . . fine.

8

HANNAH

I normally sit myself in a corner at the library, somewhere people can't look over my shoulder and watch me game. Right now, though, I think it'd be better if I turned around. I can only imagine what my face looks like.

"No, no, no! Nooooooo," I whisper to myself, mashing the keys as I fall off a floating platform to my death. Again.

[Team Chat]

PunchyTime: We have GOT to figure out a way to coordinate that section better

PunchyTime: If the tournament maps have any kind of obstacles, we will be straight-up doomed

TankasaurusRex: We need to be on voice chat

TankasaurusRex: That's how all the
professional teams play, if they
aren't all in a room together

TankasaurusRex: Can we do that?

Can we *not* do that? Ugh, I've been dreading this, but I knew it would come up eventually. I've watched enough pro gaming livestreams to know that every team-based game requires voice coordination. It's a whole other level of *real*, though. These people have never heard my voice, and I haven't heard theirs. I know in theory that they're real humans, but . . . I mean, are they? I kind of prefer the distance of typing instead of speaking.

But Josh is right. If we want to win—and I want to win more than just about anything—then we have to do this. You can't type and play at tournament-level awesomeness at the same time.

PunchyTime: I'm at the library, so
I'll have to talk quietly, but I can
jump on.

Starzzle: I'll be on in a sec

Affinity has its own built-in team voice chat, so it's really easy. Only a few seconds . . . then I activate the voice chat feature for the first time since I started playing *Affinity* a year ago.

"Uh . . . hello?" Josh says, sounding a bit thin and distant through my cheap earbuds.

I clear my throat, preparing to speak to another human for the first time since the end of the school day.

"Hi," I say, then look around. The librarians are all up at the desk or in the program room, but there's a little kid browsing the graphic novels just a few feet away. She turns to stare at me, a copy of *The Witch Boy* clutched in her hands.

"Not you," I say, holding up the microphone built into the wire of my earbuds to show her. "But that book is really good—you should check it out. The art is awesome."

She stares at me with wide eyes, then runs off without a word. I sigh.

This is why I don't talk to people.

A few seconds later, a crackle breaks the silence, followed by some muffled rustling. Then I hear Larkin's voice for the first time.

"Hey, everyone," she says in a low voice, not at all what I expected the super-energetic, always bouncing and caps-locking healer I know to sound like. This is weird.

"Wait," Josh says. "Are you here, Wheatley?"

Resounding silence.

> **EatUrWheaties:** I actually don't have a mic?
>
> **EatUrWheaties:** I can hear you, but I can't talk. Is that okay?

Everyone is quiet for a moment. Someone has to step up and be the leaderly-type person. As always, though, no one wants to be a jerk. Finally, the inevitable happens.

TankasaurusRex: It's okay for today, but we really need to be able to do voice chat by the first match. Do you think that's possible?

Thank the gamer gods for Josh.

EatUrWheaties: I'll talk to my dad about it, but yeah, probably?

STARZZLE HAS GONE OFFLINE.

"Raaaagh!" I growl, far louder than I intend to. The kid from earlier, who had at some point wandered back over, scampers away again. I can't bring myself to care right now, though. "I am going to KILL Star if she doesn't stop that. She will single-handedly lose us this tournament if she can't meet the most basic requirement, which is to *be there.*"

"It's fine, Hannah," Josh says, his voice clear and calm over the speakers. "I get what you're saying, but she only *just* told her family about her gaming. It's probably still weird. She'll get it together before the tournament."

"You sound awfully sure of that," I say, totally sounding bitter and not caring even slightly. I don't understand Star at all. We have the same dream. We both want to be professional gamers, and this tournament is the best chance we'll ever get. I can't imagine putting that at risk by doing what she's doing. Then again, I don't have a family like hers. My mom barely notices that I game, much less cares. When I had her sign the permission slip, it was right after she stumbled through the door at nine, completely exhausted after her second job. She didn't even read it, just listened to my explanation, said "I trust you, Han. Congrats," and scribbled a sloppy signature at the bottom.

"Star will come through," Josh says firmly. "Now come on, we need to practice. What should we work on today?"

One of the older librarians who doesn't like me as much wanders past and gives me the stink eye, pointing to an imaginary watch on her wrist. I shrink deeper into my seat, my cheeks heating. Yeah, yeah, whatever, I have over an hour left. I'll keep it down.

In game, I look around at all of our options. Training dummies are good for practicing DPS output. Obstacle courses are good for maneuvering and coordinating movement with abilities and spells. What we really need, though, is to practice working together as a team. Learning each other's abilities and all that.

"Let's use the practice arena. We could spar, either one on one or two versus two. Since we all play weird class combos, it would probably help us learn how our spells and stuff can work together."

EatUrWheaties: That's a good idea

EatUrWheaties: My bees need to learn teamwork

I bust out laughing, then slap a hand over my mouth before I scare off any more little kids. Wheatley is *so* weird. Total space cadet, and I *love* it.

"Well, let's get those bees of yours into the arena for a workout," I say. I scroll through the practice arena settings, find us a simple open area map, and trigger the team teleport. We all disappear from the team hall and, after a short load screen, reappear in a large forest clearing with a mossy floor.

STARZZLE HAS COME ONLINE.

"I'm sorry, I'm sorry," Larkin says, sounding stressed. "I'm here. What are we doing?"

I fill her in, trying not to feel too annoyed. I'm pretty sure she can tell, though.

"So, I was thinking," Josh says. "Maybe we should work in pairs, then switch off after a bit. So each pair can figure out what abilities each person has and how they might be able to work together in a tournament match."

"Makes sense to me," Larkin practically whispers.

"Yep, let's do it," I say much louder to spite her, earning me a glare from a dad browsing the chapter books with his kid. Oops. I wave and mouth a *sorry* to him so he hopefully won't report me.

I pair up with Wheatley first, which is . . . interesting. He doesn't say much, and what he does say is stuff like "bee-pocalypse" and "feed the bees, Hannah." It's all I can do to keep from laughing my face off as we spar first, then spend time going through our abilities one by one to think of ways we can play off of each other. Turns out we have some great ability combos.

> **EatUrWheaties:** My Lightsting
>
> **EatUrWheaties:** I fire the stinger, it does the stabby thing and shocks them with . . . electricity
>
> **EatUrWheaties:** *Shocking*, right?

I cover my face and groan. I can't tell if his jokes are so bad they're good, or just *bad*.

"So . . . meaning it does damage and leaves the target with weakened defenses?" I ask, to clarify.

> **EatUrWheaties:** Yes, that
>
> **EatUrWheaties:** Then while they're weakened, you can do a finisher

"Or if they're still pretty healthy, I use my own lifedrain to weaken them again when yours wears off. Yeah, that sounds good. Let's practice it."

It takes a few tries to get the timing down. It's hard to see when the sting hits, because the electrical zap is so faint with the graphics turned down on my ancient laptop. Eventually, though, we manage to nail it six times in a row. We'll still need more practice in the future to make it really stick, but if we can get it working in a real match, it's a powerful move.

"Thanks, Wheatley. This was fun. We ready to switch, people?" I ask.

"Yeah, let's do you and me next, Hannah," Josh says. I pop my demon wings and sail over to the other side of the area, where he waits.

"I was thinking," he continues. "For me, it's mostly about getting them to stay still for you, and only getting defensive if they manage to get some good hits in."

I bound around him in a circle, trailing waves of purple demon energy. "Agree. The more they stay still, the more I can build up my fel energy for a wicked finishing move."

Josh throws his shield at me out of nowhere, knocking me down midjump, and we start to duel. He does have a lot of lockdown abilities, but my class combo is really high mobility. Between double jumps, my demon wings, a dash, and a flurry of kicks, I've got a whole action bar full of tricks to keep me out of his stuns and slows. We work together for about twenty minutes to figure out how he can counter classes like mine, and how I can break through the defensive abilities of tanks like him. But eventually, it's time to switch.

It's time to face Larkin.

When Larkin and I finally pair up last, we fall right into

step. We've been playing together for months, so we already know each other's abilities and spells well, and the way we each tend to move. You'd think we'd be even better now that we're talking over voice chat.

But it's awkward. *Extremely* awkward.

Time to get this over with.

I pull Larkin into a private voice channel so we can talk without Josh and Wheatley overhearing.

"Look, we need to talk," I say, then fall silent. I have absolutely no idea what to say, but I'm pretty sure that's what they say in TV shows when a serious conversation is about to happen, so I go with it.

"Sure! What about?" Larkin whispers, trying to sound chipper. Can't let that throw me off, though. This needs to happen.

"You know," I snap. "The logging-out thing. Why are you still doing it? I thought you talked to your parents. They signed the form, right?"

A beat of silence. "Yeah, I turned in the form."

"So then . . . I don't get it."

There's more silence, then a sniffle. Oh my god, did I make her cry? Ugh, I am the *worst* at this. This is why I don't talk to people. It's probably good Larkin doesn't go to my school, because she would definitely hate me. There's another quiet sniffle, and then she replies.

"I'm sorry. I'm just not used to it yet. I've been playing *Affinity* in secret almost since the day it came out. It's just like playing the game, in a way. How you get your spells and abilities set up on your hotbar and your hands just get used to hitting them. It's automatic, you know? That's what it's like. The second I hear someone coming, my fingers hit Alt+F4 to close the game before my brain can catch up."

I clutch the mouse tight as I try to figure out what to say. No matter what, it's going to come out wrong, or mean, so I may as well just talk.

"We're in the tournament now. If you disconnect in the middle of the match, that puts us at a huge disadvantage for however long you're gone. They might even have rules against it, like once you're gone, you're out."

There's a faint strangled squeak, but nothing else. I continue.

"You'll lose the tournament for all of us. You need to stop. Okay?"

[Team Chat]

TankasaurusRex: Hey, I gotta go soon. Can we come back together real quick?
PunchyTime: Yeah, one sec.

I close our private voice channel, and we pop back into the main one, where Wheatley and Josh are. But I don't feel like we actually finished this. How do I know she won't just do it again next time? I will be so mad if this tournament loses me the closest thing I have to a friend. But I'll be furious if we lose, too. Maybe Lark just needs a little reminder. And this is a video game. There's no reason I have to say it in front of everyone.

[Private Message]

PunchyTime: Promise me, Larkin.

PunchyTime: Remember Glitz? Remember our goals?

PunchyTime: Going pro is possible for BOTH of us. We've dreamed about this.

PunchyTime: But I can't do it without you.

Josh rambles on in the background about some kind of strategy, but none of it sticks. I stare at the chat log and wait.

[Private Message]

Starzzle: Okay

Starzzle: I promise

Josh leaves for dinner, and Wheatley leaves to . . . go do Wheatley things, I guess. Then it's just me and Larkin in the voice chat. After an awkward moment of silence, she speaks.

"I really do promise, Han," she says quietly. "I'll stop."

"Okay," I reply, just as quiet.

She sounds sincere.

So why don't I believe her?

9

WHEATLEY

I'm still in game long after the others have logged out for the night. They all have school tomorrow. Not me.

I love being in the Hub at three in the morning, East Coast time. It's late enough that most of the West Coast players, three hours behind, have gone to bed. It's not empty, but the crowds of constantly moving avatars are gone. Most people still on at this time are either playing back-to-back matches, hanging out in their apartments, or sitting quietly in a favorite spot in the Hub while they organize their inventory, work on modifications, or whatever else.

I'm in that last group. I have a particular place I love to go to in the Nature Quarter. No, it's not *my* quarter, which would be nanotech, but I'm still drawn to this place. Not sure why. My favorite spot is all the way in the back, far enough from the Hub center that most people never bother. There's a glowing pool that swirls with what looks like liquid moonlight, occasionally streaked with fire, air, water, and earth magic. Next to it, a big tree hangs low over the pool, with long tendrils of moss nearly brushing the surface. I like to hop up onto the lip of the pool and make my avatar sit with his back against the tree. Sometimes I just watch the surface of the pool swirl around, the different kinds of magic weaving in and out.

Most of the time I do exactly what other people do: work on my character. Modifying the design of his armor, tweaking his skill and talent points, reading up on the constant tweaks Hurricane Games makes to the balance of the game. I want to stay on top of it all, make sure I'm playing my class combo to the absolute best effect. I *have* to, if I'm going to do what I'm supposed to do in this tournament.

I sit down next to my tree and pull up the armor mod window. There are plenty of practical tweaks I could make, swapping out one type of armor plating for another to make my character faster, or more resistant to damage, or whatever else. But I'm drawn instead to the more . . . artistic customization.

The more *pointless* customizations, my "dad" would say. He doesn't understand why I waste time carefully adjusting the tint of green in the wires under my skin, or the pattern of scuffing on my arm guards. I don't either, really. It's part of the game, I guess, and there's no part of this game that I don't touch. But it doesn't make me a better player, or a more powerful opponent. It's just because . . . I like it.

Is that allowed?

Truthfully, I'm stalling. I know I need to talk to my dad about the voice chat thing. I'm afraid he's going to say no,

though, and then my team will be mad, and we'll lose the tournament because we can't communicate like the others can. It'll be my fault, and they'll hate me for it.

I want my teammates to like me.

That's weird. That's not . . . normal, for me.

And it's not why I'm here. I'm here to play in the tournament. And to do that, I need voice chat.

Guess I should get this over with.

> I need to be able to chat with my team over voice during practice and matches.
>
> Is that possible?

I wait, fiddling with the enchantment effect on my bow. More glow? Too much glow? Blue instead of green? I test out a variety of changes before I end up right back where I started, just in time for Dad to get back to me.

> *We might be able to make it work.*
>
> *You'll have to be very careful, though, Wheatley. Don't talk more than you have to, or you'll ruin everything.*

My control on the color slider slips, and I accidentally turn my bow a deep blood red.

> I'll be careful.
>
> I promise.
>
> But if I don't do this, the other teams will have a major edge.
>
> We have to win, right?

I fix the color of my bow, back to bright white and green. More glow, I decide.

> *Winning the tournament is irrelevant.*
>
> *You need to make it to the final.*
>
> *Otherwise, what is the point of you?*

Right. How could I forget?

> Understood.

JOSH

GAMES

AFFINITY INVITATIONAL TOURNAMENT

WEEK ONE

64 teams enter.

32 will leave.

Watch the livestream of your favorite team fighting for their spot in the next round!

The matches are livestreamed.

I don't know how I managed to forget it. I mean, I *knew*. I watch these kinds of matches all the time for other games. But I never quite consciously thought: *Yes, our matches will be broadcast live on the internet for thousands of strangers to watch, and it's totally possible that we'll end the day in humiliated defeat, and everyone will get to see it as it's happening.* They won't hear our voice chat, thankfully, but they'll see every move we make. Every single mistake. Every time we get eliminated.

I take a deep, slow breath.

This is . . . fine.

(Fine in the way that makes me want to delete my character and hide in my closet for a week, that is.)

The four of us stand in the staging area of the first battlefield of the tournament. All the tournament matches take place on brand-new, never-before-seen maps. We can't see much from our current location, sitting behind a force field inside our base. We can still pull up the map screen, though, and see some basic details: rocky terrain, mostly, with a big wide-open area right in the middle of the map. It's a capture-the-flag map, where we'll have to fight our way across the whole field, get inside the opposing team's base, and steal their flag . . . then bring it all the way back to our own base.

I hate CTF. Ever since Brian Fulsom tripped me into a mud puddle and stole the flag from me during a real-life version of capture the flag at summer camp, I've avoided it even in video games. I'm regretting that now. I could definitely have used the practice.

The match counter hits three minutes to start, and we're still bathing in awkward silence. I tap my thumb restlessly on the space bar, making my character jump in place over and over. No one has anything to say? Thoughts on strategy? Anything? Are we just going to dive into this with no plan like it's any other match?

I have some ideas. I've done some reading.

But what if I'm wrong?

> **EatUrWheaties:** Josh
>
> **EatUrWheaties:** I believe we are all
>   waiting for you

Oh. Oh *no*.

> **TankasaurusRex:** Waiting for me to
>   what?
>
> **EatUrWheaties:** Lead us. Say something.

My stomach gives an unpleasant lurch. I was afraid of that.

> **TankasaurusRex:** Why me? Why not one
>   of you?
>
> **TankasaurusRex:** You all know just as
>   much as I do about this game, or
>   more
>
> **EatUrWheaties:** Yes, but can you
>   imagine an inspiring strategy
>   speech from me?

I snort. Yeah, okay, that would be pretty hilarious. But for all his weirdness, Wheatley does seem a little different lately. Maybe he's finally settling in and getting used to us.

> **EatUrWheaties:** As brilliant as my bees are, I don't think they are leadership material.
>
> **EatUrWheaties:** Larkin would be so excited/nervous she would ramble forever and talk way too fast. Hannah would have the strategy part, but I think she would tell you herself that she's not exactly the warm, encouraging type.
>
> **EatUrWheaties:** Basically . . . because you're good at it. We all think so.

Really? They aren't annoyed every time I try to step up and get us organized as a team? I could give them the wrong strategy. I could completely miss something that will lose us the match. I could say the wrong thing that will make them hate me.

But it's becoming clearer with every silent second that passes that they really are waiting for *me*.

"Okay," I say over voice chat, then clear my throat when my voice squeaks a little bit. "Um, I think . . . we can't let them trap us in that open middle area. It'll be super tempting to park there and just get into one-on-one fights over and over. We have to be smarter than that, though. We need flag captures if we're going to win."

"Just call me out, why don't you," Hannah snaps, her voice tight with nervousness. I bite my lip—great, I've already messed up—but she forces a laugh to take the bite out of her words. "I solemnly swear not to repeatedly punch fools in the wasteland. Promise."

"I can carry," Wheatley says. There's something off about his voice, but it's probably just nerves. I haven't heard enough of him to really know what he sounds like normally anyway. He only just got a working mic two days ago and has barely spoken.

"You're the fastest, so it's probably best," I agree. "Do we want to do two on offense and two on defense?"

Bright red letters flash up on the screen:

ONE MINUTE TO MATCH START

"That's probably safest to start with while we see what this other team is like," Larkin agrees. "You want me to run with Wheat? Or are you gonna try to tank for him?"

Why is she asking me? I don't know any better than anyone else. And honestly, I don't know what the right answer is. It's a good thing the tournament matches are best three out of five. We're gonna need that time. It would be easier if we knew what team we were up against, but the seeds are totally random. They draw up the matches the morning of and keep it secret, so we have no idea what we're up against until we meet them on the field. Makes it hard to pick a strategy.

"You go with him the first time so I can defend our flag," I say, trying to sound confident. "We can switch it up on the fly if we need to. Let us know what you're seeing as you run, though."

Did that sound smart and leaderly? If they're going to make me make these decisions, I have to have the information.

Hopefully they won't die in the wasteland before I get the chance to get it.

TEN! NINE!

Red numbers flash on the screen, counting down. I place my shaking hands on my keyboard and mouse.

Here we go. The start of our very first match of this tournament. Please, please, please let it not be horribly embarrassing.

THREE! TWO! ONE!
GO!

The force field between us and the battlefield drops, and we charge out to get a look at what awaits us. There are three twisty hallways that lead outside—the first problem that might bite us.

"Everyone pick a tunnel and let's see where they come out at," I say. Did that sound too demanding? We have to know the layout of our base if we're going to defend it, though. Thankfully, the others peel off toward different tunnels right away with no argument, and I take the one that remains. When I emerge onto the battlefield, my initial assessment of the map is turned upside down. There's a huge open area in the middle, just like we imagined. What looked like rocky areas along the sides, though, are actually huge impassable hills. You might be able to climb over and through the valleys, but it would take forever. Running across the open middle is the only way to get there.

"I have an idea," Larkin says as she and Wheatley take off toward the enemy base. "Let's hug the mountains and duck in and out of them wherever there are bushes or lower hills. I'll use my invisibility on cooldown, so hopefully they won't notice there are two of us."

"Got it," Wheatley agrees.

And they're gone, leaving Hannah and me alone at the base.

"Soooo," she says, dancing back and forth nervously. "Should we go inside and guard the flag?"

Agh, why do I have to decide this, too? What if I pick wrong? I run around both sides of the base to get a look at the outside, then blow out a breath to ease the nerves in my chest. The base is kind of divided into three sections: tall in the middle, then two lower side buildings.

"Ummm . . . how about I go inside and park on top of the

flag, and you go around to the left and Shadowblend on top of the lower roof. They'll never see you. When they run in the front, you can follow up behind them and we'll catch them between us. Sound good?"

But she's already gone, double-jumping up onto the lower roof and fading into the translucent demon form that will hopefully keep her from being spotted.

Then I follow my own assignment. I park and wait.

And it is *killing me.*

What's going on? Are we losing? Are we winning? Are things already hopeless? My stomach feels like it's full of writhing snakes. I can't take the silence.

"Updates?" I ask, my voice tight.

"We're nearly there," Larkin says. "But we haven't seen a single other player. I really hope they aren't turtling. This'll be a real short run."

Turtling: Keeping all their players at the base and forcing us to constantly be on the offensive, throwing ourselves at their very well-defended stronghold. A risky strategy for them, because at some point you have to score at least one flag cap to get the win, and if you wait too long, it's nearly impossible to catch up. But it's very hard for the other team to score, too.

"Let's take different hallways," Larkin says, and Wheatley agrees. Then it devolves into battle chatter, and my heart races at the sound of a fight I can't be part of.

"Two defenders."

"Focus fire the Surgeon!"

"My snare is on cooldown, I can't–"

"Big heal incoming–agh, interrupted, can you–"

"Where did she go?"

"She's on me, she's got–no!"

"Star!"

STARZZLE HAS BEEN ELIMINATED.

First elimination of the match. I'm gonna throw up.

"I've got the flag," Wheatley says, though he still sounds off. Stressed out, probably, since he's now the biggest target on the map. "I don't think I'm getting out of here, though."

"I can go if–" Hannah starts, but stops herself. That's a good sign. She knows there's nothing she can do. Our job is here.

Then the edges of my screen flash red, and my character hunches over.

"What?" I blurt in confusion . . . but then I see the blur darting around me. I'm stunned, completely unable to move, as a Fae Engineer alternately sprinkles me with sleep dust and whacks me upside the head with a giant wrench.

That's just . . . insulting.

It's not even a fight. A second character joins the fight, and I can't even get a good look at them before my character collapses.

TANKASAURUSREX HAS BEEN ELIMINATED.

And a moment later:

My hands are shaking so badly. As I lay on my back, staring up at the ceiling, I see my mistake.

"There's a hatch in the ceiling, right above the flag. They dropped down on my head and took me out before I even knew they were there."

"I never saw them coming," Hannah says. "I'm sorry, Josh. I'm going after them."

"No, Hannah, don't bother, they'll just–"

"I've got eyes on the flag carrier. He's a Ghost Mage. No wonder I never saw him. I have to at least try–"

PUNCHYTIME HAS BEEN ELIMINATED.

"Ugh!"

A few seconds later, just as I respawn, an urgent sound plays as a flag pops onto the screen.

RED TEAM: CAPTURE!

And things totally spiral out of control from there. The match victory condition is five flag captures or the most caps at ten minutes, whichever comes first. It's looking more and more like they're going to hit five caps with plenty of time to spare.

We never do manage to recover after the shock of that opening. We try to adjust our strategy on the fly, but the other team is really good, and we just can't seem to get a foothold. We manage one single flag cap before the other team

steals our flag out from under our defense for the fifth time with two minutes to spare.

And that's it.

Bright red letters splash across the screen:

BLUE TEAM: DEFEAT!

We lost.

JOSH

Best three out of five, I remind myself, pacing my avatar back and forth across the screen. In each round of the tournament, the first team to three wins gets to move on. Sure, we lost *badly*, but we only lost one match. The silence over the voice chat is heavy with the despair of an embarrassing loss, though. Maybe I should say that part out loud. They're probably expecting it, like Wheatley said. Here goes.

"Hey, uh . . . team. I know that was pretty bad. It feels completely awful to lose like that. But it was only one match. Let's shake it off and figure out what we can do differently this time, okay?"

There's a thump, like someone just slammed a fist down on their desk, and a quiet sniffle that makes me think someone might be crying. I kind of feel like crying, too. That loss wasn't just a lost match—it was humiliating. We got five-capped. And we only managed one capture ourselves. I take a few deep breaths to calm down and push away the buzzing panic in my chest. We have to do better. But how?

On the screen, big red numbers begin their countdown:

two minutes to match number two. We only get five minutes between matches, which isn't much time to talk strategy. We have to be quick.

"Real fast, let's talk team composition. We know they had a Fae Engineer and a Ghost Mage. Did anyone get a look at the other two? Did I hear something about a Surgeon?"

Larkin and Hannah make general "I dunno" kinds of sounds, but surprisingly, Wheatley speaks up.

"I remember them from the team profiles," he says. "The other two are a Robo-Titan and a Song Surgeon. They're one of the best teams in the tournament, so we shouldn't feel bad for losing a match."

That might be the most words I've ever heard Wheatley speak in a row. And I'm super thankful for them. That's a great point.

"How can you possibly remember that when there are sixty-four teams?" Hannah says in awe.

"WHO CARES. Wheatley is amazing. Thank you, kind sir, for your supermemory. So, what can we do with that?" Larkin says.

The red numbers blink to get my attention: one minute remaining. My heart speeds up.

"Okay, okay, so obviously what we did last time didn't work, so let's just throw spaghetti at the wall and see what sticks, try a whole bunch of different strategies. I'll try to run the flag this time and see if my extra survivability makes a difference. Hannah and Wheatley, wanna hide in the bushes out front, let them run in and get the flag, then take out their carrier?"

"Worth a shot," Hannah says.

"Sure," Wheatley agrees.

"And I'm with you, Tankasaurus, your faithful healer," Larkin adds. "Hey, it can't go *worse*, right?"

The ten-second countdown begins.

"Okay, we've got this, team. We're in this tournament because we're good players. We can win this."

Then the buzzer sounds, the force field drops, and we're off.

It goes . . . better. Ish. For a while. We manage three caps to the other team's four, but they run down the clock at the end, turtling up on top of their flag.

We lose.

Again.

It's two to zero. One more win for the other team, and that's it. We'll be out of the tournament in the very first round.

I look around at my teammates. Larkin, sitting motionless on the ground, so weird for her. Hannah twitching back and forth with nervous energy. Wheatley standing stock-still, the glow on his bow shifting between shades of blue and green.

This can't be our last match together. Not now that we're really starting to be friends.

I can't let that happen.

"Okay!" I say, forcing some cheer into my voice. "We did better that time! Right? So this next match—it's ours. We've got this one. What do you want to do? Let's refine our strategy."

Hannah runs circles around me, jumping. "I haven't carried the flag yet. Can I try?"

"Sure, why not," I say. "Everyone okay with that?"

"I got your back!" Larkin chirps. Wheatley doesn't say anything, but that's normal. Okay, so . . . something inspiring. What can I say? We're never going to win unless we believe we can. I have to help them *believe*.

I clear my throat and go for it. "All we have to do is get one more cap than them and run out the match timer. We don't have to five-cap. We just have to stay one step ahead. We can do that. We know our weirdo classes, and they don't know what to expect from us. I doubt

they've ever faced a Demon Puncher or a Nano Ranger before. So let's pull out all the weird tricks we have, all the abilities they don't expect us to use, and throw them off. Right?"

"Right! Let's wreck them," Hannah says, her voice full of pure determination.

"I can't wait for them to see a Mender bringing an entire moon crashing down on their heads," Larkin says.

"My bees are hungry," Wheatley adds. Which, cool.

THREE! TWO! ONE! GO!

And it *works.*

Turns out, Hannah is a perfect flag carrier. Her demon wings give her a perfect speed boost, and her double jump takes her out of most melee players' range, so she can't even be hit. Larkin crows with pure gamer joy every time she casts Moonshot, literally pulling a moon out of the sky to crush our opponents. I can see the enormous glowing white orb crash onto the battlefield all the way from our base, where I run patrol: through the tunnels, onto the roof, around the back, into the bushes, constantly changing location so they never know where I'll be. Wheatley switches up his strategy, too. First, he sets an electrical trap on top of the flag and hides nearby. Then he finds a vantage point overlooking the base and targets the other team before they even get there, picking them off one by one. It's like we're a different team.

The other side never manages to figure us out.

THREE! TWO! ONE!
BLUE TEAM: VICTORY!

There's a muffled squeal over the mic, then:

Starzzle:
    Ahhhhhhhhhhhhhhhhhhhhhhhhhhhhhhhhh!
Starzzle: Sorry, I can't yell at home,
    but AHHHHHHHHHHHHHHHHHHHHHHHH!

"YES!" Hannah shouts, then whispers far away from the mic, "Sorry, I'm sorry, I'll keep it down."

"Still playing at the library?" I ask.

"No other choice. I'll keep my victory dancing to a minimum. Now let's do that AGAIN."

"Yes. Again," Wheatley adds.

And we do.

Our second win is even better. We change up strategies, not wanting to get predictable. We keep Hannah as carrier but experiment with sending a group of three over, and with leaving our flag undefended altogether. By the end of the match, it's five caps to two . . . in our favor.

BLUE TEAM: VICTORY!

"Eeeeeeeeeee!" Larkin screeches, then cuts off sharply and switches to a whisper. "I mean . . . *eeee!*"

"The bees say good job, everyone," Wheatley says. Right. Thanks, bees.

"One more match," Hannah says, sounding out of breath. "One more match, one more match, we've *got this!*"

"We've *definitely* got this," I say, forcing confidence into my voice.

In reality? I have never been more nervous in my entire life. I'm about to see my lunch for a second time, all over this keyboard.

It's two to two. Whoever wins this next match moves on to the next round of the tournament. Half of all the teams playing today will be cut. I don't want us to be one of them. I *need* for us not to be one of them. If we're cut in the first round, it'll just prove to my parents that there's no point to me spending time on this game. My friends, my team . . . we'll drift apart without the tournament to keep us together. It'll prove to my parents that they were right about them, too. Not real friends, after all.

It's not true, though. We are real friends. And gaming is worth my time. We're going to make it to the next round.

We *will.*

"Want to change things up?" I ask the others. "Or should we stick with what we've been doing?"

"My dad always says, 'If it ain't broke, don't fix it,'" Larkin says.

Hannah laughs. "Agree. Besides, I think we've found our rhythm now. If we need to adjust on the fly, we can. Right?"

"I concur," Wheatley says. Who uses the word *concur?*

"Okay." I blow out a nervous breath, then stand up and shake out my hands and arms, willing the tension away. "Good luck, everyone."

"No luck needed," Wheatley says. "The odds are in our favor. We will win."

"I like your confidence," Larkin says.

The ten-second countdown begins.

I sit back down, settling my right hand on the mouse and my left over the WASD keys.

Hannah starts running into the force field, her avatar jogging in place against an invisible wall. She'll break free in three . . . two . . . one . . .

GO!

Hannah's character shoots forward the second the force field disappears, and Larkin flickers right after her, disappearing from the flag room and reappearing next to Hannah. They're a well-oiled machine now, perfectly coordinated as they make their speed run across the field. We keep up with our strategy for the first five minutes, but something isn't working. We're at four caps, but the other team is right on our heels at three, and they're getting much more used to our abilities and combos. Our elimination count is up, too. This match is *way* too close.

"Incoming!" Hannah says, hopping like some kind of demon rabbit toward the entrance to our base, a glowing blue flag stuck to her back.

Then she's ambushed.

"I got you!" Larkin says, weaving a quick Heal-Over-Time spell onto Hannah before pummeling the other team with her Starfall ability. Hannah's health ticks slowly up, but not fast enough to keep up with the beating she's taking.

Then they turn on Larkin, too. In barely two seconds, she's frozen and silenced, completely locked down. Unable to attack or cast a heal or even run away.

"I'm coming to help," Wheatley says, sending in his swarm of nano-bees and following them up with a volley of raining arrows. It's not enough, though.

PUNCHYTIME HAS BEEN ELIMINATED.

STARZZLE HAS BEEN ELIMINATED.

Shoot. Wheatley picks up the dropped flag to continue the run, but it's not looking good.

"Wheatley, just focus on surviving, I'm coming to—"

EATURWHEATIES HAS BEEN ELIMINATED.

"No!" I yelp.

Then the whole team turns and charges at me.

I run, but it's no use. A moment later, their cap count ticks up.

RED TEAM: CAPTURE!

4

My pulse accelerates. We're so close to losing.

But we're close to winning, too. Whoever gets this next flag capture wins the match, and the round.

"Okay, new strategy," I say. "We're gonna zerg rush, all four of us, straight at their flag and leave ours undefended. We grab their flag, we come back as a group, and when we encounter their flag carrier, all four of us focus fire them down. If our carrier dies, whoever is closest, pick it up and run for it."

That's all I have time to say. We all respawn back at our base within a few seconds of each other.

And we make our run.

My heart pounds so loud in my ears I can barely hear the team chat.

"Split up," Hannah says, veering off to one side with Larkin. "If they see all four of us together, they might adjust."

"Good point," I say, and Wheatley and I peel off to the other side of the map. Wheatley uses his Nanocloak ability to turn invisible whenever it's off cooldown, but I'm a big lumbering tank. I'm not supposed to be quick or stealthy. If they see me, then . . . Hulk smash, I guess.

"They sent two over," Larkin reports. "Their Robo-Titan and Ghost Mage just ran by. Not sure if they saw us."

"So their Fae Engineer and Song Surgeon are still in or around the base," Wheatley says. "Strategy?"

"Run right up the center tunnel, all four of us," I say, putting on the one and only semipathetic speed boost I have. "Strength in numbers is the only way we'll win this one."

We meet up at the front and charge in like a stampede of glowing, glittering cattle. The two in the flag room don't stand a chance. We completely steamroll them. Wheatley locks down the Engineer with his stun while we pummel the Surgeon, then turn back to the other just as the stun breaks. Hannah grabs the flag and books it out of there, the rest of us hot on her heels.

"Stay together, stay together," Wheatley says, but more like he's talking to himself, reminding himself not to screw up. I take up the chant in my own head as the other two opponents come charging down the field with our flag. *Stay together, stay together, don't screw up, stay on target.*

"We have to take them out quick," Hannah says, sounding breathless. "Before the other two can respawn and come at us from the other direction."

"Carrier first," I say, just as their flag-carrying Titan comes into range. I slam him with my shield and stomp a glowing red rune into the earth, slowing his movement and reducing his damage as long as he's standing on it. Larkin lays down a big glowing circle under us just as the carrier's escort joins the fray.

"Eat your cookies," she says, meaning stand on the circle and get those tasty, tasty heals.

"Shouting," I warn her. My Defensive Shout ability comes off cooldown, and I hit the key for it, making my character smack his sword against his shield and roar. It directs half of all damage done to my allies at me instead. My health drops alarmingly fast, but Larkin is a pro, on it in an instant. She throws several Heal-Over-Time spells on me that heal a little bit of my health every second, smoothing out the incoming damage. A quick single heal and I'm topped off, so she turns her focus back to the others. Wheatley leaps into the air and blows one of his big offensive cooldowns, Hornet Sting. His swarm circles over his head, shooting out red bolts of pain into each opponent. Hannah leaps in with a flurry of punches, then winds up for her big finishing move, Infernal Drop. With a quick charge, she double-jumps as high as she can, then heel-drops right on their flag carrier's head.

He crumples to the ground, the flag glowing at his feet.

"Get it!" all four of us shout simultaneously, even Wheatley. I throw my shield up to avoid getting interrupted and click on the flag. The progress bar fills over one second, then two . . . then the flag disappears, back at our base.

This is our chance.

"Run!" I shout into the mic, shaking with pure adrenaline.

Hannah breaks off from the group and sprints for our base, using every trick and speed boost she has. The rest of us pummel the poor Ghost Mage, and the second he drops, I turn back toward the enemy base.

All three of our living opponents are racing toward us.

"Larkin, escort Hannah! Wheatley, crowd control!"

I glance down at my bar to see which stuns, snares, and other movement-stopping abilities are off cooldown. The other team's Engineer tries to double-jump over our heads to get at Hannah, but I throw my shield before she can get too far off the ground. It slams into her and leaves a glowing orange rune hovering over her head, dazing her. She'll never catch up with Hannah at that speed. Wheatley sends his full swarm at the next player to arrive. The bees glow bright yellow as they form a cyclone around the Robo-Titan, suspending them in midair for two and a half precious seconds. We pull out every trick we have: Wheatley's electrical snares, my ground pound runes, wide-area damage abilities, anything we can throw at them to keep them from getting past us. It's three against two now, though, and my health is dropping fast.

"We can't hold them any longer!" I say, my voice ragged and breathing harsh. We're so close, so close!

"Cap it!" Larkin shouts.

BLUE TEAM: CAPTURE!
5

All the action stops, our characters frozen in mid-move.

I hold my breath until the words splash bright across my screen.

BLUE TEAM: VICTORY!

12

AFFINITY TOURNAMENT HEATS UP
WITH ELITE EIGHT SHOWDOWN
By: Alisha Washington

The *Affinity* Invitational Tournament is three weeks deep, and if the way we're all glued to our screens is anything to go by, it's proven that there's plenty of demand for an *Affinity* Pro League. Hurricane Games went all out, pulling some of the biggest eSports stars and streamers in to provide often hilarious commentary over the matches. Each round is made up of five 4v4 matches on a brand-new, never-before-seen map (some of which, it is rumored, will be added to the game in a future patch), so no one can say what's coming in the Elite Eight.

Week One began with sixty-four teams on a CTF map. The Weird Ones barely pulled through that round, having been pitted against one of the best teams in the tournament right out of the gate. They pulled off an impressive and nail-biting win, though, earning a fair number of new followers in the process. The rest of the Elite Eight teams pulled through that round without a scratch, though that certainly didn't hold for the next two rounds.

Week Two featured the thirty-two remaining teams

on a wartime fantasy-themed capture point map. Three equidistant castle control points were separated by difficult terrain, and victory went to the first team who managed to capture and hold two of the three castles for one minute. Phantom Gryphon Party, The Night Pixies, and The Weird Ones dominated this round, with Electric Virus and The Iron Overlords barely scraping by into the next week. The Crimson Hackers were the ones to watch in Week Two, though, with their incredible three-minute, three-cap win.

Week Three stirred up fierce controversy as Hurricane Games introduced a completely new twist: an escort map where one player from the escorting team had to actually be seated inside the vehicle for it to move . . . thus rendering that player unable to contribute to the fight. Every team struggled with this one, and the first two matches were throwaways in almost every case while players figured out the new mechanic. By the end, each of the remaining eight teams had figured out some sort of novel strategy that put them over the finish line. Though the shake-up wasn't popular with every *Affinity* fan—or tournament player—this map was a true test of each team's creativity and strategic thinking.

"If that threw you off," Hurricane Games representative Mark Chowdhury said, "then just wait until next week. I'm already mourning our social media mentions. Please don't @ me."

These eight teams have been truly tested, ensuring that the remaining matches will be some of the best *Affinity* content we've ever seen.

Click on a team name to see a full breakdown of members and tournament highlights ahead of the Week Four matches.

The Crimson Hackers (68,998 followers)

Electric Virus (35,590 followers)

Fun Club (46,250 followers)

The Iron Overlords (38,674 followers)

The Night Pixies (52,258 followers)

Phantom Gryphon Party (87,193 followers)

The Weird Ones *(55,458 followers)*

Wicked Nation (39,874 followers)

THE WEIRD ONES

Team Profile: They have the youngest average age of any team in the tournament, but that isn't stopping them from blazing a strong path to the finals. The unusual class combos that give this team their name also give them an advantage, since few players have ever faced these particular combos in a match.

TankasaurusRex (Josh)

Tank: Rune Knight

Age: 12

Signature Move: Shield Slam

Best Tournament Moment: Week Two, Match 3—Staying alive for a whole forty-five seconds while soloing three opponents through frankly ridiculously pro use of cooldowns, maneuvering, and battlefield control.

PunchyTime (Hannah)

Melee DPS: Demon Puncher

Age: 13

Signature Move: Infernal Drop

Best Tournament Moment: Week One, Matches 3–5—Basically every single flag carry was super well executed, but the Infernal Drop right before the final cap of the round was *epic.*

Starzzle (Larkin)

Healer: Star Mender

Age: 12

Signature Move: Moonshot

Best Tournament Moment: Week Two, Match 1—
Somehow (and I'm still not sure *how*), this Mender managed to run back and forth between two capture points,
keeping both teams alive for ninety seconds straight,
long enough to cap both points for the win.

EatUrWheaties (Wheatley)

Ranged DPS: Nano Ranger

Age: 13

Signature Move: Hornet Sting

Best Tournament Moment: Week Three, Match 2—
Pioneered the Hop and Drop technique during the Week
Three escort map, hopping straight up out of the driver's
seat to fire off an AoE attack around the vehicle, then
dropping straight back down to drive forward. Rinse
and repeat on cooldown. Genius!

Add THE WEIRD ONES to your Follow list
for email updates and exclusive content.

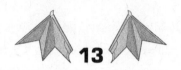

13

HANNAH

We are on. FIRE.

The week leading up to the quarterfinals has been intense in ways I totally didn't expect. It feels like every single gaming website in existence is running stories on the tournament, the teams, and even individual players. The first time I stumbled across a blog article entirely about *me*, I completely freaked out. Larkin wasn't online, so I sent her a very caps-lock-y email with the link.

Then, I'm not gonna lie . . . I totally took screenshots and copy/pasted the text into a document to save it. It's my first-ever coverage as an almost-professional gamer. My mom's not gonna scrapbook it, so I have to save it somehow.

The *Affinity* official website is even hosting player profiles, now that it's down to only eight teams. They asked for a real-life photo from each of us, which I did *not* love. I agonized over it for two days, sending Larkin five different photos to help me pick from. I finally ended up having the teen librarian take a thousand new ones with her phone and send them to me so I could have something actually up-to-date, instead of last year's school photo. They aren't great, to be honest, but at least I look like me: ballcap with the Alliance starbird logo from Star Wars, hair pulled back, serious expression while I focus on the game in front of me. While I totally hated having to put my photo out there, I also secretly loved the profiles finally being public . . . because I get to see what my teammates look like.

Josh looks exactly like his avatar, but also *super* familiar, like when you see someone you've never talked to at school out at the mall or something. Larkin looks like her email profile photo, though I can actually see the blue streaks in her hair in this larger photo. Wheatley looks absolutely nothing like I pictured, though. He's super pale and has red hair with a tiny bit of wave, just long enough to get in his eyes. There's something odd about the photo, but I can't put my finger on it. Maybe that it's professionally done, unlike the smartphone photos the rest of us submitted?

Once the profiles went up, we all started getting bombarded by requests for interviews and fan mail, of all things. I can't log in to the game without getting a million private messages, so I eventually had to put myself in Do Not Disturb mode. We spend the week training, though it's hard to imagine what we might be up against. They could throw another total curveball at us like last week, with a twist that completely upends any familiar strategies. Or, it could be a straightforward team-based free-for-all. All we can do is keep practicing together, honing our abilities, and staying focused.

Not like I have anything else going on in my life to distract me. After the library closes and I have to go home, all I do is sit around drawing *Affinity* fan art. I try doing homework sometimes, but my mom is never around to help me, so I just get frustrated and end up doodling in the margins. It's all so pointless. I don't understand anything, and it makes my brain feel like a paranoid squirrel running away from a hawk, so most of the time I don't bother. Even if my home internet won't let me play *Affinity*, sometimes I log in just to watch people run around in the Hub and listen to the music. It's calming somehow.

Better than nothing, I guess.

The day of the match, my mom drops me off at the library later than usual because she has a Saturday shift at work. I desperately hope someone isn't already parked in my usual tournament spot. It's bad enough that I have to play in public with people all around me. If I have to find a new spot, I'll feel so *weird,* and people might walk behind me, which I hate, and . . .

As soon as I walk through the door, though, I know something's wrong.

The library is *packed.*

Not that it's not normally busy. The library is really well used, always filled with families, people working on their laptops, teen volunteers, and so on. But there are banners, and balloons, and tables set up all over the library. I glance over to my usual tournament seat, only to find it taken over by a guy in his midthirties with a giant stack of books on the table next to him and a line of people in front. I look up at the banner over the entryway.

LOCAL AUTHORS FESTIVAL
Saturday, April 9th, 9am—5pm

Oh. No.

Ms. Hayley, the teen librarian, spots me standing there and comes over with concern in her expression.

"Hannah, are you okay? What's wrong?"

I guess the fact that I'm totally about to start crying in the middle of the library is super obvious.

"I . . . I really need the internet today? It's really, really important. But it doesn't look like . . ."

I trail off with a despairing look at the occupied tables, now clearly packed with authors signing books.

Ms. Hayley frowns but taps her lower lip in thought. "You go to Parker Middle School next door, right?"

Yes, because school is definitely what I want to be thinking about now, thanks.

"Yeah?" I snap.

"Don't they have weekend computer lab hours for students without internet to do homework? Maybe they wouldn't mind if you played your tournament match there."

My head whips up, my eyes wide. "Wait, how do you know about the tournament? Do you play *Affinity*? Was I really super obvious?"

She ticks off each point on one hand. "No, I don't play *Affinity*, but yes, I *am* a gamer who reads gaming news sites, and yes, you were super obvious."

Whoa. I don't think I've ever met an adult gamer before.

I know they exist, obviously–I've destroyed a few of them in this tournament so far. But Ms. Hayley is like . . . a real person. Awesome.

"We can talk about it some other time," she says, shooing me out the door. "I don't want you to be late meeting up with your team before the first match. Head over to the school, and have them call me if they give you any problems. I'll vouch for you."

If I were a huggy kind of person, I would definitely tackle-hug this librarian right here, right now.

"You are the *best*," I say instead, adjusting the strap of my laptop bag on my shoulder and running for the door.

"Good luck! And don't run!" she calls after me, so I slow to a very intense power walk until I get out onto the sidewalk.

The school is literally right next door, so I run for the front office entrance as fast as I can without dropping my laptop. When I burst through the door, the guy at the front desk looks up in surprise.

"Hannah, what are you doing here?" he asks, putting down the book he was reading. Something with an orange-pink cover and a girl with a jousting lance on the front.

"I need to . . . use the . . . computer lab?" I say between panting breaths. His confusion clears, and he turns to his computer.

"Okay, you're checked in," he says, then hands me a sticker from the tiny printer next to him. "Wear this pass on your shirt and show it to the lab monitor when you get there."

"Thank you *so* much, seriously!" I say, then sprint down the hall.

"And don't run!" he calls after me.

Yeah, okay. Back to intense power walking, fine.

I burst into the lab, and everyone looks up at me. There are maybe seven kids there, probably people who live outside of town where there's barely any internet service. At the front of the classroom, a bored-looking Black girl with her nose in a college physics textbook sits with her boots up on the desk.

"Pass?" she drones.

I point to the sticker on my shirt, and she jots down my name on a clipboard, then waves me away and gets straight back to her homework. O-kay. Right, then.

I park myself in the back corner, as far away from the other people as I can get, and set up my stuff for the tournament. It's gonna be so weird playing here, but I'll have to make it work. No other choice, really. I open up my laptop and launch the game while I plug it in, get out my earbuds, and get my wireless mouse out of my bag. When I glance back up, my chat log is blowing up.

[Team Chat]

Starzzle: Where is he?

Starzzle: Jooooooosh

EatUrWheaties: Should you try calling him?

My heart crawls up into my throat. What's going on with Josh? He's never late. In fact, he's always really early.

Starzzle: Hannah, there you are omg

Starzzle: I was starting to freak out
a little

PunchyTime: I told you I was going to
be late. The library was packed,
though, so I had to find a new
place. What happened with Josh?

Starzzle: I have no idea. I haven't
seen him all morning.

TANKASAURUSREX HAS COME ONLINE (APP).

Starzzle: THERE HE IS

Starzzle: JOSHUA MIDDLE NAME, YOU ARE LATE

Starzzle: WHY ARE YOU IN THE APP
INSTEAD OF IN THIS GAME WITH US

TankasaurusRex: Is now really the time
to fish for my middle name?

TankasaurusRex: My internet went out
at home. I don't know what to do.
I tried getting our match delayed
until the afternoon, but they
said no. We either play with three
people or forfeit.

Yeah, neither of those options is okay. He needs to find someplace fast. The match starts in twenty-two minutes, and we're required to accept the teleport to the tournament grounds five minutes early.

PunchyTime: Josh listen

PunchyTime: Does your school do weekend lab hours? Like, for kids who don't have internet at home?

PunchyTime: Mine does, and that's where I had to go today, the library was NUTS

TankasaurusRex: Hannah you are a GENIUS

TankasaurusRex: According to google, my school DOES have an open lab

TankasaurusRex: brb

TANKASAURUSREX HAS GONE OFFLINE (APP).

He's cutting things awfully close. All the anger and irritation are building like steam in a kettle inside me, and I'm sure Josh is about to explode with stress, too. If Ms. Hayley hadn't suggested the school to me, I'd probably be panicking right along with him. I'm going to lose my mind if I just sit around and stare at my character until he gets logged in at his school, though.

PunchyTime: Let's just start warming up until he gets here

PunchyTime: We should be ready to go no matter what

PunchyTime: I hope he gets here though. He's going to hate himself so hard if he doesn't.

Starzzle: Yeah, I would be absolutely panicking if I were Josh. He's probably being terrible to himself.

Starzzle: Wheatley, are you and the bees ready to go?

EatUrWheaties: The bees are go for launch.

EatUrWheaties: But Josh will be here. We don't need to worry.

I wish I was as confident as Wheatley. I always assume things are going to go wrong until they prove otherwise.

I find my teleportation crystal in my inventory and click it to beam myself up to our team hall, where Larkin and Wheatley are already running the obstacle course and practicing on training dummies. I join in, running some courses to warm up my fingers, but the lab around me is so distracting. The next row up, two kids are laughing and watching YouTube videos. Someone else leaves, slamming the door super loud, and someone else opens the door barely a second later, inexplicably carrying an entire computer tower. I have to focus, though, have to block it all out and concentrate on the upcoming match. The kid who just came in is in fierce negotiations with the lab monitor about something, but I turn up the volume on the game sound and let the repetitive sound effects of my character kicking, punching, and casting spells fill my ears.

There's a *thunk* on the end of my table, and I turn to look. The boy with the computer tower is setting the thing up at the end of my row, moving at a frantic pace. So obnoxious. Did he have to pick here of all places? I'm about to turn back to my practice, to see if Josh has logged in yet . . . then the boy at the end of the row looks up.

What?

No.

WHAT?

NO WAY.

"Josh . . . ?"

14

JOSH

"You said it was an emergency, Josh!" my dad shouts as he throws the front door open, holding it for me as I stagger through. I've got my entire computer tower in my arms, cords dangling free and threatening to trip me. That would really be the icing on the absolute garbage cake that today has been. I had nightmares all night about the quarterfinals, woke up at three in the morning, couldn't go back to sleep, broke a dish and got yelled at over breakfast . . . and then our internet went out.

I don't know what else I was supposed to do. My mom's team is launching some new project, so she's working today. I tried calling her office, but they

said they couldn't track her down because she's all over the building meeting with her teams this morning. We don't have any other family in the area, and I obviously don't have any friends who live here, so I had no choice. I had to call my dad.

How was I supposed to know he had a job interview? Not like he ever tells me anything.

"I'm sorry, Dad," I say for the thousandth time as I put the computer in the back seat and buckle it in. "But this *is* an emergency. My whole team is waiting on me. Our match starts in fifteen minutes."

The school is only five minutes away, but we'll be cutting it very close. My breath is coming faster now, but not from the running and carrying. I'm starting to panic.

"There is no universe in which a *video game* qualifies as an emergency, Josh," Dad says with as much disgust as he can possibly muster. "Do you have any idea what I thought when I looked down at my phone and saw *ten* missed calls from you?"

"Murderers," I mutter.

"Or injury," he says. "Or kidnapping. Or who knows what. The only reason to call someone ten times is because your life is in danger. I nearly ran over a member of the hiring committee on my way out of the parking lot."

"Then they *definitely* wouldn't have hired you," I say, then shut my eyes and groan. Stupid thing to say. Damage control. "But they will! I'm sure your interview was great! You always manage to get hired so fast every time we move."

Did I save? I rush around the car and squeeze into the back on the other side, one hand resting protectively on my computer while my dad slams the driver's-side door and starts the car. He takes *forever* checking his mirrors and pulling out of the driveway, but I don't dare say a word. One more wrong move and he'll pull me from the tournament altogether. He'd probably be happy about it, too.

I pull up the *Affinity* app while my dad drives (*so slowly*) to the school, but I log in with invisible mode on. I don't know why I don't want any of my teammates to talk to me right now. I stare at their names on my friends list and notice my thumb shaking over the screen. My breath burns in my lungs, and my eyes feel heavy, like they're full of hot tears waiting to fall. That's all I need right now—to completely lose it and have a panic attack right before the match.

My thumb hits Wheatley's name without me really telling it to.

> **TankasaurusRex:** Is everyone really mad at me?
>
> **EatUrWheaties:** No. Worried, mostly.
>
> **EatUrWheaties:** They know how much you're probably beating yourself up right now.

Dang. I wipe my eyes on my sleeve quickly before my dad can see. Wheatley is right, of course. I kind of hate myself for getting into this situation. For not calling my dad as soon as the internet went out. For not planning ahead for problems like this.

> **TankasaurusRex:** I don't know how I'm
> supposed to lead the team today,
> after all this.
>
> **TankasaurusRex:** I can't just pop in
> five minutes before the match,
> so close that I nearly made us
> forfeit, and take charge.

My heart speeds up, and I realize how true what I'm saying is. This is exactly what's making me panic right now. Not just being late for the tournament. Losing my friends. Losing their trust.

> **EatUrWheaties:** You can do exactly
> that, though.
>
> **EatUrWheaties:** We're all waiting for
> you to get here and lead us into
> the match. Even the bees.
>
> **EatUrWheaties:** You aren't "taking"
> charge. We're giving you
> charge.
>
> **EatUrWheaties:** . . . I'm not sure
> that's the right way to say that,
> but do you get what I mean?

I really hope he's right, because the school is in view. Thirty seconds out. I have maybe two minutes to get my head in the game. I could argue, or question Wheatley, or tell him all the reasons I think I'm a terrible leader and someone else should take over. But the quarterfinals are minutes away, and there's no time. So instead, I just say:

TankasaurusRex: Thanks, Wheat.
TankasaurusRex: You're a good friend.
TankasaurusRex: See you in game soon.

I log out of the app and stash my phone right as my dad pulls to a stop in front of the school office. Before I can leap out of the car, he turns around and braces his hand on the passenger seat to give me a hard stare.

"This is the last time, Josh," Dad says, his voice grave. "I will not be bending over backward for this video game tournament again. Do you understand?"

"Yes," I say. I don't doubt it.

"I'm picking you up in two hours. Be out here and ready."

"Yes, Dad."

He stares at me for a long, uncomfortable moment. It takes everything I have not to fidget . . . or just give in and run full tilt down the hallway to the computer lab. After what feels like an eternity but is probably only about five seconds, he looks away. I get out of the car and grab my computer, and then he drives off.

I know this is going to come back and bite me. But I can't think about that right now.

I head inside, check in at the front office, then run toward the lab as fast as I can while not dropping my precious computer. Please let the lab monitor be cool and let me do this, *please*. I don't think I can stand any more icing on this garbage cake. My team needs me.

And I need them.

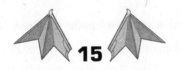

15

HANNAH

"Josh? Is that you?" I ask again.

The boy's head whips around. Then his eyes go wide with surprise.

"Hannah? Seriously?"

I gape like a fish for an embarrassingly long time. My brain is straight-up broken. My worlds are colliding. Josh, TankasaurusRex, *Affinity* player, team captain, THAT JOSH, is sitting at the end of my row.

"Do you go to school here?"

"Yeah," he says cautiously. "I started at the beginning of this semester."

"Ah-hah!" I slap a hand down on the table, then wince and wave to the lab monitor with a quick "sorry." But I KNEW Josh's picture looked familiar. "That's why I didn't recognize you right away. You're new. And . . . and we don't have time to talk about any of this, because our match starts in *eight minutes*. How can I help?"

He hands me his half-unzipped bag. "Can you unload my stuff? Mouse, headset, cables–"

He doesn't even need to finish. I'm on it. Within a minute, we have his rig completely set up and plugged into one of the lab computer monitors. I move my stuff over to be closer to his. This has to help our chances, right? Being able to work together in person? There's a team of two wives on one of the remaining eight teams, and I always thought it was kind of unfair that they got to sit next to each other and game. Huge advantage. But now I get to work with Josh during this round, so the advantage suddenly doesn't seem so unfair.

[Team Chat]

PunchyTime: You will NOT believe this

PunchyTime: Josh is HERE

PunchyTime: Like, right next to me, a flesh-and-blood human being. We go to the same school.

Starzzle: WHAT

Starzzle: NO

PunchyTime: YES

PunchyTime: He's logging in now

EatUrWheaties: The odds of that are . . . not much? Wow.

PunchyTime: RIGHT???

TANKASAURUSREX HAS COME ONLINE.

TankasaurusRex: Hi, I'm so sorry, I'm finally here. Let's hop on voice?

"It is deeply weird seeing you talk on the screen when you're right next to me," I comment, glancing over at Josh.

"And I feel deeply weird doing it, so . . . I dunno, go team, I guess," he says. I huff a small laugh at that, and he looks . . . shy, or embarrassed or something?

"Are you two really sitting right next to each other?" Larkin says in my ear.

"We are," Josh says, seating his headset more comfortably over his ears. He glances over at me with self-consciousness, then visibly pulls himself into leader mode. I try to make it easier on him.

"Okay, Captain," I say over the mic. "Five minutes to the match. Any words of wisdom for us?"

Josh blinks at me, owlish. "Captain?"

"Obviously," Larkin and I reply in unison.

A box pops up on both of our screens:

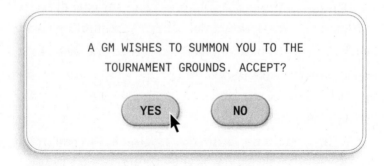

A GM WISHES TO SUMMON YOU TO THE
TOURNAMENT GROUNDS. ACCEPT?

YES   NO

"Okay, then. Let's see what the map tells us," Josh says.

We both click YES in perfect sync. His computer loads way faster than mine, though. His character appears in the waiting area of the next tournament map after only three seconds of loading time. I sit there for a solid twelve seconds before my old hand-me-down laptop finally agrees to load me in. When I look over at Josh's screen, he already has the map pulled up and is studying it, so I do the same, not wanting to look lazy.

But . . . I don't understand what I'm seeing.

"Uh . . . Lark? Wheatley? You guys are here, right?" I ask.

"Yeah . . ." Larkin replies, sounding wary. "But I don't see you or Josh. Are you here?"

"Yes," Josh replies, then sits back with a hand in his hair. "We're in two completely separate arenas. Bring up your map."

Oh.

The map shows two long rooms on either side with a giant blank space in the middle. At one end of one room, there are two dots representing me and Josh. At the end of the other room are Larkin and Wheatley. There's no way to get from one arena to the other.

"So, what is this, then?" I ask, drumming my fingers anxiously on my keyboard.

"It appears to be a 2v2 versus 2v2 map," Wheatley says, sounding entirely too calm.

"You say that like it's a thing," Larkin says, much more on my level of panicky. "But it's not. Not in *Affinity*, not in *Overwatch*, not in literally any game I've ever played."

I shake my head, disbelieving. "How is this supposed to be balanced? Are we going to respawn in the same pairings every time we die? Did they choose which class combos were going up against each other, or is this random?"

"Yeah, I don't understand this," Josh agrees. I look down and see his leg bouncing restlessly a mile a minute under the desk. "The game is tuned for 4v4 play. How is this supposed to be a fair test of our skills?"

"Perhaps it's not supposed to be fair," Wheatley says, to resounding silence. What do you even say to that? What's the point of a tournament if it's not designed to be fair, for the best team to win not because they're lucky, but because they're *good*?

Josh shakes himself and sits up straighter. "Okay, well, it kind of doesn't matter right now. This is what's in front of us. We can think about the rest of it after we've won."

"I guess Hurricane did say this week would be 'controversial,'" I say. "We gotta roll with it. Any thoughts, wise leader?"

Josh shoots a look over at me, but surprisingly, he doesn't blush or shift in discomfort. He's transformed from the bumbling kid juggling computer parts into a cool, calm team captain. The constant leg-bouncing is the only outward sign of his nerves.

"I don't think there's anything we can really do," he says. "There's no strategy here. The battlefield is a giant empty room, as far as I can tell. And like you said, we have no way of knowing whether we'll even respawn in the same pairs. I think this is a test of our knowledge of each other as much as it is about how well we know our own class combos. I think we just have to . . . go with it."

There's silence over the voice chat for a long, despairing minute. Clearly none of us are super excited for this "test." We don't have a choice, though.

"Okay, a repeat of Week One it is, then," I say to break the quiet.

Josh hums his agreement. "Yeah. First few minutes are a throwaway while we figure out what's going on. After that, we regroup."

With only two minutes left until match time, Wheatley and Larkin start going over the ways they can work together in this situation. I do the same with Josh, trying so hard to play it cool while also feeling like I'm about to crawl out of my own skin. It's hard to concentrate over the low-level constant anxiety in my brain. Fortunately, I don't have long to wait. Let's rip this Band-Aid off.

THREE! TWO! ONE!
SINGLE ELIMINATION—GO!

A three-minute timer appears at the top of the screen with no explanation.

Wait . . . what?

"Wow, way to drop *that* on us at the last possible second," Larkin says.

"For real," Josh agrees. "So, stay alive, basically. Got it."

Okay, no throwaway match, then. Single elimination means there's no respawning. When you die, you're dead until the next match starts. No room for mistakes. And the timer is . . . what, exactly? Whoever can eliminate the most players from the other team in three minutes? Ugh, this is so frustrating, not knowing what's going on. I can feel myself getting angry again, and that never leads to my best play. I don't want to embarrass myself in front of Josh, though, so I take a slow breath in through my nose and focus.

Josh and I tentatively creep out of our starting zone and into a lush forest overgrown with vines and moss. It'll be hard to see anyone coming in all this.

"What do you think?" I ask him.

"Should we do a quick loop around the map to see what's here?"

"Sounds smart to me."

We hug the left wall and start off toward the other team's starting zone, weaving around trees and through underbrush. There's no hiding a giant Rune Knight in shiny armor, but I try to use my Shadowblend to go nearly invisible and stick to the bushes as much as possible. If they think there's only one of us, a single player roaming the map alone might get overconfident and try to take on Josh. They'll be in for a rude awakening.

We barely make it halfway up one side before Josh is ambushed.

"What do we have?" I ask, immediately blowing my cooldowns to work on taking the girl out. If there's no respawning, there's no reason to hesitate, and her teammate will be here any second. Demon Strength makes my fists glow purple as I unleash my biggest attacks: a flurry of fast punches, a big double-handed slam, and my signature heel-drop finishing move. She's already at half health, but that doesn't mean we can get overconfident. She's dangerous until she's eliminated.

"What is this, a Runefist? Funny," Josh says, and I snort. It's like a combination of our two characters: Josh's runes affinity and my martial artist teknik. Or, it would be funny if she hadn't just punched a Rune of Paralysis into my face.

"I've got you," Josh says, guarding me while the stun wears off and retaliating with a stun of his own. He lands a few solid hits with his sword, but he's built to protect, not to dish out tons of damage. Not like me. The second the paralysis wears off, I hit my highest damage finishing move . . .

. . . and get stunned *again* before it has a chance to hit as our other opponent comes racing onto the screen. I wasted *all* my fel energy on that move, and it didn't even land. I slam my hands down on the tabletop and growl in frustration. The other player is a healer, and all I can do is watch as half the damage I just did is healed up. Josh slams the healer with his shield to interrupt the next one, so it's not all undone, but it's still obnoxious.

"Sorry I couldn't interrupt the first one," Josh says. "Shake it off, it's fine. They should be out of stuns now."

He's right. The new healer, a Fae Scholar, isn't a class combo with many crowd-control abilities. We should have a good twenty seconds before we have to worry about getting stunned again.

"Focus on the healer?" I ask.

He says something back, but even though he's sitting right next to me, I can't hear him either in person or over the headphones. Larkin and Wheatley's chatter is so distracting I can barely hear myself think. Finally, I rip my right earbud out with one quick motion.

"Everything okay?" Josh asks.

"Just can't hear you over them, and what's happening to them has nothing to do with us. I can't help them, so it's just noise."

At that, Josh adjusts his headset so the ear closest to me is uncovered. "Fair enough. Yes, healer. Let's take him out."

Of course, with my earbud out, I suddenly notice that there are people standing behind me. Watching. I can't pay attention to them right now, though. We're still being attacked.

"What team is this?" Josh asks.

"Fun Club," Wheatley responds instantly.

Someone snorts, and we all bust out laughing. Well, Wheatley makes a tentative sort of "ha, ha?" noise, but close enough. It's a funny name.

"What do we know about them?" Larkin asks.

"They aren't very fun?" I say as the Runefist punches *another* Rune of Paralysis into my face, way earlier than we expected. How short is the cooldown on that? Way overpowered–Hurricane Games needs to fix that. Josh keeps me from getting completely destroyed, but we're going to need heals soon if we're going to live. Of course, the timer is already at one minute, so it may not matter for much longer.

"What *else* do we know about them?" Larkin asks again.

Encyclopedia Wheatley comes to our rescue, as usual.

"They're the second-youngest team besides us," he says, then pauses for a long moment to fight, I assume. "They're all thirteen, fourteen, or fifteen. They've mostly gotten paired against weaker teams, so no one has any real idea how good they are."

"Lucky us, we get to find out!" Larkin says with sarcastic cheer.

"Just get one person down per side, at least," Josh says. "No idea how this works, but it can't be a bad thing to end the match with more of us than of them, right?"

"Sound logic," Wheatley says, and Larkin whoops as they do something cool that I can't see.

SKULLAZ HAS BEEN ELIMINATED.

"Nice, good job, good job!" Josh cheers.

I'm determined to get this healer down before the time runs out, even if it means enduring more Runefist shenanigans. We need to isolate him somehow.

"Shield wall?" I ask. Fortunately, Josh catches on quick.

"Wall going up," he says. Then his character hoists his shield up high and slams it down between us. Josh and the Runefist are on one side. The healer and I are all alone on the other.

"You are *mine*," I mutter as I unleash everything I've got on the poor guy. The Runefist doesn't even try to face down Josh alone, clearly smelling the doom about to befall her teammate. She dashes to run around the edge of Josh's wall, but she's too late. With one last burst of quick punches, the Scholar falls to the ground.

NOTYOURHEALBOT HAS BEEN ELIMINATED.

So satisfying. I love it. I turn, winding up my next attack for the Runefist even though the timer's about to run down. Maybe we'll get lucky with some solid critical hits. We get her down to fifteen percent, but our time is up.

THREE! TWO! ONE!

I lean back and take my hands off the keyboard, shaking them out before the next round.

But the end-of-match message never comes.

Josh, the Runefist, and I all disappear. A second later, we all reappear in a tiny circular arena. For a moment, we all

stay totally still, waiting for a new countdown or something. Then I notice the Runefist is still at fifteen percent.

"The match is still going!" I shout. "Focus fire the Runefist!"

A crackling electric arrow zips past me and strikes the Runefist just before I land a huge glowing punch. She hits me one last time, but with her healer gone, she doesn't stand a chance.

IAMSAARA HAS BEEN ELIMINATED.

I whirl around. Sure enough, that arrow came from Wheatley. The whole team is back together, facing down the lone remaining member of Fun Club: their ranged DPS, a Green Sorcerer. He is *so* dead. He puts in a good effort, kiting Josh around as he tries to dodge Wheatley's and Larkin's attacks. But he's lost track of where I'm at, poor guy, and he backs right into my fully powered-up Demon Strike. Demon wings sprout from my shoulders as I rear back, then slam both fists into either side of his head.

LEAFY HAS BEEN ELIMINATED.

BLUE TEAM: VICTORY!
PERFECT WIN!

Behind me, our spectators burst into cheers. Even the lab monitor has wandered over and offers me a fist bump.

"Perfect win!" Larkin crows. "That's a new one!"

I grin. "Assuming that's because we took out all four of

them without losing anyone. We absolutely *wrecked* them, you guys!"

"Okay, now we know," Josh says. "Eliminate whoever we can in our individual 2v2s, then whoever is left gets teleported to the center arena. We've *got* this."

We've definitely got this. And we rock the next two rounds just as hard.

Best three out of five? Forget it.

We only need three.

THREE! TWO! ONE!
BLUE TEAM: VICTORY!

"YES!"

Josh and I both throw our arms up at the same time, then turn to each other for a double high five.

"We're in the Final Four!" Josh says in disbelief.

Our spectators clap for us, offering fist bumps and congratulations. It is utterly embarrassing, suddenly being the center of attention from all these people who would normally never talk to me at school. But we actually deserve it. We did it.

One step closer to the pro league.

I leap all over the screen, mashing the space bar in excitement, and jump over to Larkin's avatar to run some circles around her. This deserves some serious celebration.

But she disappears.

STARZZLE HAS GONE OFFLINE.

☆ 16 🌙 ☆

LARKIN

Caught.

It's all over.

I kept my promise to the team. I didn't Alt+F4 and quit the game the second my dad walked in.

So. He saw.

He stood there and watched me as I played the last minute of the match. When I made that last saving play. When I played bait so Hannah could get that final win. He saw it all. And now?

It is so, so quiet in here.

I stare down at the keyboard, refusing to look up and meet his eyes. I don't know how to talk about this. How to defend myself.

"You wanna tell me what this is about?" my dad says, tapping my phone where the match commentary was playing just a moment ago. "I thought I heard the name Starzzle. Isn't that the name you used to make us call you when you were—"

"Yes," I say, frantically trying to cut off his mortifying recap of my little-kid pretend games. Yeah, I was a magical fairy. So what.

"Yes?" he prompts, waiting.

I take a deep breath.

And I tell him everything. How I love to play. How I'm one of the best in the country at healing, and how I got my invitation to the tournament. I even tell him about Glitz and my dream of going pro. That's the part that scares me the most. More than admitting just how often I've been breaking the household ban on video games. Even more than admitting I forged his signature. It feels a little like floating, letting go of all the things I've been hiding. But also a little bit like my heart is on the outside now, where something terrible is sure to happen to it.

When I finish, he stays quiet for a long minute.

"Well, Bug," he says finally. "I'm going to have to talk to your mom about all this, obviously. Is the tournament over for the weekend?"

I nod miserably.

"No more game for the rest of the weekend, then, at the least," he says with finality. "I think that's fair, don't you?"

Honestly, no. I don't think it's fair at all. Yeah, my brother screwed up a few years ago, and he couldn't balance his gaming with school. But that's *him*, not me. Have I ever done anything to prove that I can't be trusted? Other than lying about gaming for the past few years, I guess. But still! It's the struggle of younger siblings everywhere–the pressure that comes with your parents' expectations that you won't repeat your sibling's screwups.

And I try. I really, *really* do. I get straight As at school. I do band and drama, and my teachers say I'm good at them. I go to language and music camps in the summer, already thinking ahead to college applications. I help take care of the animals, and water the plants, and do everything else I'm asked to do. I just have this *one thing* that's for me, that I love *so much*. I don't feel like I'm my full self without gaming.

But I don't expect them to understand that.

"Bug? Did you hear me?" my dad asks.

"Yeah," I drone. "I guess that's fair."

What else am I supposed to say? Hopefully if I obey, they'll be softer on me and at least let me play out the rest of the tournament before they take the game away entirely. So I can "focus on what's important." It doesn't matter that this is important to *me*. It never does.

My dad says something else, but I don't hear. I'm all in my own head, imagining all the worst-case scenarios as I slowly stand up, walk past my dad, and retreat to my bedroom.

What if I can't finish the tournament?

What if I let everyone down?

What if this is the end of my professional gaming dreams?

I flop facedown on my bed, my phone on the covers next to me, and just try to fall asleep.

My phone buzzes constantly for about twenty minutes

before finally falling silent. It's probably Hannah messaging me in the *Affinity* app, or the team chat blowing up as they all discuss the win and our chances in the Final Four. *Their* chances, that is. Who knows if I'll be able to play with them.

I ignore it. I ignore the call for dinner. I ignore my sister begging me to play Ticket to Ride. (Board games are allowed, but I just don't feel like it right now.)

Eventually, though, the guilt gets to me. And the hunger. I sneak down to the kitchen to grab a bowl of leftover pasta, then manage to dodge my sister and get back in bed. My phone vibrates ominously . . . but no new messages. Just pestering me about all the ones that came in earlier. I open up the *Affinity* app and tap the chat tab and see exactly what I suspected: twenty-eight missed messages from the team chat, and eight from Hannah privately. I feel awful. I flip over to my friends list to see if anyone is online right now.

Friends List (1 online)
EatUrWheaties

I hesitate. Of all the people on the team, Wheatley isn't exactly who I would normally pick to talk to about things. But I feel like I'm drowning in this mess, and I need to confess to a teammate. In some ways, Wheatley might actually be the perfect person. He's the one I know least. He's not as much of a friend as Hannah is. She'll be so mad at me. And he's not our leader, like Josh is. He'll be massively disappointed in me. Wheatley might be the closest thing to neutral as I can get.

He messages me before I can make up my mind.

> **EatUrWheaties:** Hey Larkin. Are you
>   okay?

Well, that makes things easier. I tap to open up the message thread . . . and it all comes pouring out.

> **Starzzle:** I am SO sorry about earlier
> **Starzzle:** I'm the worst
> **EatUrWheaties:** You are not the worst.
>   What happened?
> **Starzzle:** Is everyone super mad at me?

There's a longish pause, which doesn't bode well.

> **EatUrWheaties:** They aren't thrilled
>   exactly. But you played out the
>   match. That's the most important
>   thing.
> **EatUrWheaties:** I believe they will
>   forgive you.
> **Starzzle:** They? But what about you?
>   Are you mad?
> **EatUrWheaties:** Oh

EatUrWheaties: No, I'm not mad

EatUrWheaties: I don't really get mad?

Starzzle: Well, that's a relief.
Thanks.

Starzzle: Though you might change
your mind once you hear everything.
Time for my big confession.

Starzzle: I . . . didn't actually get
the permission slip signed.

EatUrWheaties: But you're playing in the
tournament. I thought you had to?

Starzzle: Yeah. I chickened out of telling
my parents about my gaming. I faked
my dad's signature and sent it in.

Starzzle: I KNOW, it's a terrible
thing to do, and I really regret
it. I wish I'd been honest from the
start.

Starzzle: But then they might have
said no, and I never would have
gotten this far in the tournament
with you all. So . . . no, I guess
I don't regret it.

Starzzle: I just really hope my
parents don't hold my stupid
decision against me and keep me
from finishing the tournament.

> **Starrzle:** We're in the Final Four, Wheat
>
> **Starzzle:** FINAL FOUR
>
> **Starzzle:** Did you ever imagine we would get this far?

There's another long pause, during which I imagine him sitting in front of his computer, trying to figure out how exactly to tell me I'm horrible. Maybe I overwhelmed him with too much confession. But instead, he answers my question.

> **EatUrWheaties:** I didn't really have any expectations about how far we'd get
>
> **EatUrWheaties:** I just wanted to do my best
>
> **EatUrWheaties:** And
>
> **EatUrWheaties:** This might be . . . weird of me? I'm not so good at telling sometimes. As I'm sure you've noticed.
>
> **EatUrWheaties:** But I actually really want the bonus armor customizations the final two teams get. I don't really care about the other prizes.
>
> **Starzzle:** That's not weird. We all get different things out of playing the game.

Starzzle: Hannah gets really into the customization and crafting, too. She says art is the only thing she's good at outside of the game. Is that what it's like for you?

EatUrWheaties: Not exactly

EatUrWheaties: It's like . . . I don't normally get to have any input about what I look like

EatUrWheaties: And in game, everything can be changed

EatUrWheaties: I get to figure out what I want and just . . . do it

Starzzle: What, does your school have uniforms or something?

Another eternal pause, even longer than the last one.

EatUrWheaties: Do you really think your parents will keep you from playing?

O-kay. He clearly doesn't want to talk about his situation, whatever it is.

Starzzle: I don't know. I've never kept something from them like this. I always do what I'm supposed to do. This is the first time I've really messed up.

Starzzle: I really hope that even if they don't want me to pursue gaming professionally like I want to, that they'll at least let me finish the tournament.

Starzzle: I don't want to let you all down. You'll hate me.

Starzzle: But I don't want to disappoint my parents, either

EatUrWheaties: I won't hate you

EatUrWheaties: You can't control who your parents are, or what they want you to do

Starzzle: What about your parents? What are they like? From what you've said before, it sounds like your dad is really involved in your gaming. That must be nice, to have someone who understands.

EatUrWheaties: It's not quite . . . how it sounds

EatUrWheaties: He's kind of . . .

overinvolved? He sort of makes me
play. And I enjoy playing with you
all, and I'm glad to be on this
team. But it's still weird.

Starzzle: Makes you play? How? Why?
I can't imagine my parents ever
WANTING me to play a game

EatUrWheaties: It's not how it sounds.

EatUrWheaties: I'm not what I seem,
Larkin. I'm

EatUrWheaties: Uh-oh

EATURWHEATIES NOW HAS STATUS DO NOT DISTURB.
NO MESSAGES WILL BE DELIVERED.

Oh no. I hope I didn't get him in trouble. His dad sounds
really strict. And kinda weird, if I'm honest. I flop back against
the pillows and let my phone fall to the bed. I can't quite bring
myself to read the team messages or Hannah's PMs yet.

My backpack sits leaning up against the foot of my bed,
a notebook hanging half out of the main pocket. I bend forward and grab it, flipping it open to the back pages. I don't
let anyone see this notebook, and this is why. Every page is
covered in printed-out pictures of female and nonbinary professional gamers. For each one, I've written out their stats:
age, country of origin, games of choice, tournaments won.
Most of the pictures are of Glitz, though.

I stare down at my most recent addition, a picture of her larger-than-life avatar from the tournament announcement. I hate that I missed it. The idea of getting to play in the same professional league as her, in a game I love so much, is . . . It almost *hurts* with how bad I want it. I lay my hand over the picture, close my eyes, pour all of my fierce hope into the page.

Please let my parents understand.

Please let me finish out the tournament.

Please don't let this dream be dead.

17

WHEATLEY

I didn't know I was capable of feeling guilty. But here I am, looking back over my chat log, at all the things Larkin told me. Confessed to me, really. She told me things she hasn't even told the rest of the team yet. Something that could get her in serious trouble if someone at Hurricane Games found out. She was so honest with me.

But I'm not being honest with all of *them*.

I think back to the first day, when I was assigned to their team and all I knew about them was the profiles they posted on the tournament forums. I had no idea how to act around them. I thought I would just show up, do my job as best I could, then be done. But somehow, we've become . . . friends? They seem to consider me a friend, at least. Of all the things that I thought might happen during this tournament, that was one thing I never even considered.

Friends don't lie to each other, though. Friends don't hide everything about themselves and show you a fake front.

I'm in our team hall, sitting in a dark corner with my back against the wall, looking out over our practice space. We've been too busy actually practicing in it to customize it at all, and it's been bothering me. I want to change the color of the walls and add a design of some kind to the floor. I have plenty of in-game money I'd be happy to spend on new stuff. But it's not really my place, is it? I can't just redo everything without the team's input, and it feels weird to ask. It's the exact sort of project that would help me feel better right now, though.

PUNCHYTIME HAS COME ONLINE.

Hannah's avatar fades into existence in the center of the hall. I check the clock even though I know exactly what time it is. It's much later than Hannah's usual gaming time. The library she plays at is closed.

PunchyTime: Hey Wheat

PunchyTime: What are you doing up?

EatUrWheaties: Ha, I'm always up. How are you online? Isn't the library closed?

PunchyTime: Yeah, but I couldn't sleep. I have internet at home, it's just that crappy $10/month internet they give broke people. I can submit my homework and check email, but that's about it.

> **PunchyTime:** I definitely can't play
>   any matches, but sometimes I like
>   to log in just to zone out and play
>   around with my gear, redesign my
>   look, you know.

Oh. Wow. It's weird to have something *so* in common with someone. I don't think that's ever happened before. The late hour seems to make Hannah less rough, a little more open. Maybe that's why I tell her.

> **EatUrWheaties:** I do the same thing.
>   It's . . . peaceful?
> **PunchyTime:** YES. Makes my brain feel
>   less alksdjhflaskdjf all the time.
> **PunchyTime:** Also, it's just really nice
>   to not have to deal with people

Oh no. Does she—

> **PunchyTime:** Not that you aren't a
>   person!
> **PunchyTime:** God, this is why I don't
>   talk.

> **PunchyTime:** I just mean you aren't
> like OTHER people. You're . . .
> quiet, I guess?
>
> **PunchyTime:** More like, you don't seem
> to expect me to BE a certain way.
>
> **PunchyTime:** Does that make sense?

I pause, processing that for an alarmingly long time. I am . . . feeling things about it. I don't know how to put it into words. I think Larkin would call it "big friendship feels." That would sound strange coming from me, though. Instead, all I say is:

> **EatUrWheaties:** I think the same thing
> about you.
>
> **EatUrWheaties:** You don't seem to mind
> that I'm . . . weird.
>
> **EatUrWheaties:** You just let me be.

And . . . neither of us quite knows what to say next. There's a long, long pause. I can tell it's getting awkward, so I blurt out the other thing that's on my mind.

> **EatUrWheaties:** Hey, do you want to
> redesign the team hall?

EatUrWheaties: I've been wanting to, but I thought if I just did it without talking to anyone it would be . . . not good.

PunchyTime: Yes

PunchyTime: PLEASE

PunchyTime: If I have to look at these boring white walls for another day I will SCREAM

PunchyTime: . . . I actually designed a team logo for us, but I haven't shown anyone. It's probably bad. But if you like it, maybe we can put it on the floor in the center of the arena, or on the wall or something?

She walks over to a long blank wall and opens the customization menu. Her character swipes around on holographic menus for a while . . . then a design appears on the wall. At its center is a red rune (a quick search online tells me it means "oak tree") that appears in several of Josh's abilities. On either side are simple purple demon wings. Arching over the top are five stars, and under the bottom are five tiny bees, both in the electric blue that Larkin and I share.

It's all of us, rallied around our leader. It's perfect.

> **EatUrWheaties:** Make it bigger. And put a big stripe across the center of the wall, end to end.
>
> **EatUrWheaties:** Can you send the file to us as a decal we could add to our armor?
>
> **PunchyTime:** I guess that means you like it.

Oops. I guess I should have said.

> **EatUrWheaties:** Yes, it's perfect for us. I think Josh and Larkin will love it.
>
> **EatUrWheaties:** Can I tell you about some other ideas I have that I think will match?
>
> **PunchyTime:** Yeah, go for it!

She might regret that. I have a *lot* of ideas.

We spend over an hour tweaking colors, rebuilding features, and spending way too much in-game money on new items for the space. Hannah drops offline a few times when her internet fails, but she always comes back, ready to keep going. It's honestly the most fun I've had in the game . . . maybe ever. I like playing matches, and I know my dad would think this is pointless, but I don't care right now. I don't care what I'm *supposed* to be doing, or what my *purpose* here is. I like this. I like having friends. I like having fun. I wish I could just keep doing this and forget about the tournament.

Then I remember, and all those feelings just . . . go away.

This is all fake. If Hannah knew me, *really* knew me, she wouldn't be hanging out with me, making art out of our team hall. If Larkin really knew me, she wouldn't have told me her secrets. And if Josh really knew me, he wouldn't talk to me when he's nervous about being our leader. They would all just . . . stop.

As our project starts winding down and Hannah starts talking about going to bed, I have a dangerous thought. I almost told Larkin. I could tell Hannah. I should stop her before she goes. Tell her everything.

I should.

PUNCHYTIME HAS GONE OFFLINE.

But I don't.

It's probably for the better anyway. Hurricane would pull me from the team and ruin the tournament for everyone. I barely dodged my dad catching me earlier when I was about to tell Larkin. Too close. Way too close.

I teleport down to the Hub and head for my favorite spot to think. That guilty feeling swells bigger and bigger. What do people do in this situation? I can't fix the real problem, so . . . maybe I can make it up to them somehow? How can I help the team and make this better?

I'm running through the Hub when I see another player with a tournament participant flag next to their character name, and it hits me. I can research the other teams we'll be playing next weekend in the Final Four! If I learn everything about them, then no matter which team we face next week, we'll have a strategy to take them on.

This is it. I can do this.

I open a new browser and dive into the research. There's a ton of match footage on YouTube, so many articles all over the internet, profiles on eSports websites to study, and more. At the beginning of this tournament, there were too many teams to keep track of. Now, with only three other teams left, it only takes me a single night to compile it all into a document of my own.

TEAM: Wicked Nation

TANK: Nano Mecha

HEALER: Potion Scholar

MELEE DPS: Song Monk

RANGED DPS: Star Ranger

STRENGTHS: Number-one-ranked ranged DPS in the

game, most players are high mobility, very effective tank

WEAKNESSES: Low on crowd-control abilities, lack of Heal-Over-Time abilities, friction between team members

ANALYSIS: This is the team we should most be hoping to face. Of all the options, they are the ones who

> *Wheatley. Stop it.*

I close the document instantly, but it's too late. I've been caught, just like Larkin.

> **What am I doing wrong?**

Maybe playing dumb will work?

> *You know what you're doing.*
>
> **Why is it wrong, though?**

I can't stop myself from asking. I truly don't know.

This is part of being on a
team, right? This is what all the
players are probably doing this
week. Preparing for the semifinals.
I thought I was doing well.

You aren't there to help
them win the tournament,
Wheatley.

You are there to observe.

Stop interfering in the outcome
and focus on your observations.

The fact that we're having this
problem is a very good sign,
in a way. But it needs to stop.
Do you understand?

I don't. I really don't understand at all. But there's no
arguing with my "dad." It's pointless.

I understand.

Good. Keep talking to your
teammates. Keep learning.

After all, the tournament could be
over for you this week.

Even if you make it to the finals,
it's only two more weeks total.

> *Make the most of every second.*

Ah. Well.

I guess this is what sadness feels like.

> **I'll never talk to them again after the finals, will I?**
>
> *You know you won't. There won't be any need. This was always going to be temporary.*
>
> *Now, try to focus. Are we clear?*

I pause for what feels like a long minute but is probably only a few milliseconds.

> **Yes, sir.**
>
> *Good. I'll be watching this week.*

I wait for a few minutes to see if he'll say anything else, but it looks like that's it.

Honestly, that was plenty.

Tomorrow, I think. Tomorrow I'll email that document to the others. I can't work on it anymore, but they may as well get some use out of it. My dad will probably notice me sending it, but oh well. A lot of the time, it feels like he knows what I'm thinking anyway. He won't be surprised. How does he expect me to *not* try to help my team win?

In the meantime, I sit down in my favorite place to sit and work on my modifications. He can't bother me for doing that. Maybe I should change my entire color palette for the semifinals just in case it's our last match ever. Maybe I'll ditch the electric blues and greens in exchange for red, black, and gold. See what everyone makes of that.

And while I work on redesigning my look, I think about the document. The Night Pixies. Phantom Gryphon Party. Wicked Nation. One of those teams will be our opponent this weekend. The only thing standing between us and the final. Between Josh, Hannah, and Larkin and their pro gaming dreams.

I won't get to be with them for that. I doubt I'll be allowed to play ever again after the tournament is over.

But if it's going to be my last match ever, I'm going to go out with a bang.

JOSH

The Final Four tournament nerves were bad enough on their own. I'm already three hundred percent more terrified than in any other round.

Then the doorbell rings.

"Hannah, welcome!" I hear my mom say from the front of the house. "It's so nice to meet you!"

"Um, you too?" Hannah replies.

Hannah and her mom both humor my mom with some polite small talk, though I know it's not really their style. Hannah doesn't talk about her mom much. I get the feeling that it's a bit of a sore topic. All I've been able to gather is that Hannah really likes her mom, they're really similar, and they used to be close. Now the only time she sees her is in the car when she's getting dropped off somewhere. No wonder Hannah plays *Affinity* so much. As much as my parents get on my nerves, I think it would be worse to be alone all the time.

I should really go greet them at the door or something. That seems like the thing my dad would tell me to do, at least, so it's probably the proper thing. But I can feel the weight of my mom's hopes and expectations from here. Yes, I finally have a friend, she's at our house like a normal friend would be, we're playing video games but we're doing it in person together so it's somehow less bad, et cetera. My dad and I are still barely speaking since the match last week, and I'm pretty sure he thinks Hannah is a bad influence. I don't really care what he thinks, though. We've made it this far. We're pro quality. We deserve to be in the tournament, and Hannah deserves to be here as my friend.

I have my computer set up on our dining room table for today's match, which is great because it means there's room for Hannah to set up right next to me. We can both plug directly into the router instead of relying on wireless internet, too, which is a great bonus. In the Final Four, we need every advantage we can get. My parents never would have let me set all this up if Hannah weren't coming over, but there's nowhere in my room for two people to sit at a desk and play. The perks of having parents who are desperate for you to make friends.

Hannah comes into the dining room in what I've started thinking of as her Hannah uniform: a video game–related T-shirt, a ball cap with her hair pulled through the back, and a backpack covered in pins and patches. She's exactly the kind of person I would normally be too nervous to talk to at school, even though the *Affinity* patch on her bag is a safe signal. She seems way too cool. But this week, we talked at school several times. We even sat together at lunch, when normally we would both go hide on our own: her in the art room and me in the library. I guess if nothing else comes out of the tournament, at least I've made a real-life friend.

"Hey," she says, sitting down next to me. She puts her laptop on the table and lets it boot up while she unloads her stuff with quick, jerky movements. She's probably nervous, too. But is she nervous about the tournament, about being at my house, or both?

"Hey," I say back. "Ready for this?"

"Kinda have to be, I guess." Her avatar loads into the game right in front of mine, where we logged out together last night. Before we can start warming up, though, Marvin lumbers in from the kitchen, sniffs at Hannah's leg, then slumps on top of her feet.

"He smells," I warn.

"He's perfect," she corrects, leaning down to pet his scraggly head. "Aren't you, buddy? I am a friend to all dogs."

I make a face. "Tell me that later when he farts and it wafts up in the middle of a match. It's enough to distract you to in-game death."

My parents mostly leave us alone as we run the obstacle course and pummel the training dummies with Larkin and Wheatley, once they arrive. They're both unusually quiet and have been all week. I don't know what to do about it, though. Larkin told us what she did. Her parents are letting her play out the tournament to fulfill her obligation to us, but that's all I know. And I have no idea what's going on with Wheatley, but then again, none of us ever do.

Instead, I talk about the thing we're all here for: the Final Four match. We go back over the data Wheatley collected for us and plan for the worst-case scenario, with my parents wandering by and occasionally peeking over our shoulders. Every time they walk past us my shoulders climb up next to my ears, and it's like there are ants crawling all over the back of my neck. Are they listening to me being the captain of this team? Do they hate it, or does it make them think a little better of me and gaming? Hannah doesn't seem to mind them at all, at first. She's probably used to strangers at the library walking all around her, so this is no big deal. Every time my mom talks to us, though, or rests a hand on my shoulder, Hannah looks away.

Once we've crammed in as much speculation as we can fit into our brains, I lead us through some drills to practice new strategies we've developed over the past week.

Then, way too soon, it's match time.

Hannah and I both lean back in our chairs to stretch and shake the tension out of our hands, then turn to each other and laugh. We probably look ridiculous, holding our hands out to the sides and flopping them around like the world's worst jazz hands. The two-minute warning on the screen kills the laughing pretty quick.

The Final Four. The semifinals.

If we win this match, we're in the final. The top two teams. The eight best players in *Affinity*.

No pressure.

"Okay, everyone," I say, trying to force something solid and confident into my voice. "Call out your observations as you see them. We've got no clues on this one. From the super-helpful map, it could be just about anything."

And by *super-helpful,* I mean it's completely blank. We have no idea what's out there.

Hannah snorts. "Yeah, frustrating to not even know what kind of match we're playing. Capture the flag? Free-for-all? Cap and hold? Escort? They could have at least given us a clue."

"I think our odds are good, though," Wheatley says. "We've all seen the data."

Wheatley does seem to love his data. But I have to admit, he made a really good case. By the time he finished explaining all the research he'd done, even I was feeling a bit more confident about today's match.

"Hey, if Wheatley's bees say we've got this, then I believe them," Larkin chimes in with a bit of her old cheer. "Should we stick together until we know what we're doing?"

The ten-second countdown starts, and my heart hits the gas pedal hard. The four of us stand shoulder to shoulder in front of the door to the arena, Hannah's new team logo decal on our chests. Ready to go.

"Yeah. Stick together," I force out. I lay my shaking fingers over the WASD keys.

THREE! TWO! ONE!

GO!

As soon as the force field drops, I see why the map was all blank.

We are literally in space.

Floating. In space.

A pink shimmery comet zips across the sky in front of me, and I hear a half-panicked laugh escape me without my permission.

"WHAT." Hannah does not sound happy. "What is THIS? We're just supposed to learn how to fight in three dimensions on the fly?"

Oh *no*, she's right. It won't be that bad for Wheatley and Larkin, since they're ranged classes. But for me and Hannah, as melee characters, we somehow have to figure out how to stay close enough to our targets to hit them. Easy enough when you have solid ground under your feet. In space, there is no ground. There is no *down*.

And we still don't even know what our goal is.

"Any clues on the match type?" Larkin says as she goes zooming by.

"I believe this is a team-based free-for-all," Wheatley says, calm as ever. "There's an elimination counter at the top of the screen now."

He's right. It wasn't there while we were waiting in the ready room. It must have appeared as soon as the match began.

"Okay. Easy enough," I say, trying to regain some calm and project it to the rest of the team. "We can manage that. What do we have to work with?"

"Asteroids," Hannah says. I see her camera swinging around on her screen as she scans the zone. "Kinda

scattered all around. That's about the only cover we have available."

"Not the only," Wheatley says, gliding past me. "Look in this direction. See the light?"

I squint and lean closer to the screen. Nothing. What is he looking at?

"Right here," Hannah says, pointing to her own monitor. I lean over and look where her finger meets the (kinda gross and smudgy) laptop screen.

Ah, he's right. It's hard to see because the object is painted black, but occasionally it drifts past a star, making the light disappear for a second.

"What are those, space junk or something?" Larkin asks. "I think those are a less obvious option. The asteroids are basically begging for someone to hide behind them."

"Agree," Hannah says, then glances at me for guidance.

I scan the horizon for incoming enemies and run through some possibilities in my head. "Okay, here's a thought. To start off, let's all four pile behind a piece of space junk. Wheatley, you can wander out. Then as soon as they see you, lead them back to us."

"Then we evaporate them," Larkin says in a voice that says *evil villain rubbing their hands together*.

"I love it," Hannah says, and takes off for the nearest piece of space junk without another second's thought. The rest of us follow, and before long, Wheatley comes flying back with a Fae Rogue hot on his heels.

"Stun lock," I say, bashing the guy with my shield so he

can't move for two seconds. Hannah follows it up with a stun of her own, then Wheatley, so by the time the guy can move, he's already an inch from . . .

KARAX HAS BEEN ELIMINATED.

"Yesss, nice! Good job!" Larkin says, spinning in a circle. "Again?"

"Again," I say.

It only works three times, but it's enough to give us an early lead. It also gives Hannah and me a chance to ease into melee fighting in three dimensions. A minute and a half into the ten minutes and we're ahead 3-0.

In the middle of our fourth attempt, after moving to a new hiding place, we discover the flaw in our plan.

STARZZLE HAS BEEN ELIMINATED.

"Uh-oh," Larkin says ten seconds later, after she respawns.

"Why uh-oh?" I ask in the middle of taking vengeance on Larkin's behalf.

"I didn't spawn back at the start," she says.

Uh-oh.

I pull up the map in the middle of channeling a bubble shield, just for a second, and catch a quick glimpse of Larkin's dot all the way on the other side of the map. An elimination must mean that we respawn in a totally random spot on the map.

Before long, both teams are completely scattered around the map and it turns into a true free-for-all.

"Find Larkin," I shout as I block an incoming spell from the Fae Sorcerer, who snuck up on me. Larkin is the squishiest of us all, definitely not able to survive by herself unless she's up against the other team's healer alone.

"I have her," Wheatley says.

"And I have their healer." Hannah cackles next to me, and there's a flash of purple light on the horizon.

IAMALEXIS HAS BEEN ELIMINATED.

And that's the one that puts us over the top. We hit twenty points and win the first match with two minutes still on the clock, solely on the strength of those three early eliminations.

It won't work again, though.

"Okay, everyone, that got much closer at the end. We need to come up with a new tactic. Any ideas?"

The next match countdown starts as soon as the last word is out of my mouth, though. Two minutes.

"What?" Hannah says, looking over at me with wide eyes. "What happened to our five-minute break?"

"I guess they're trying to test how we think on the fly," Larkin says. She sounds nervous. Understandable. Healers have giant targets painted on their backs in every match, but in a free-for-all, it's worse than ever.

"Okay, okay, think think think." I don't mean to say it out loud, but it comes out anyway. What can we do?

"This team is the Night Pixies," Wheatley says. "Their players are a Star Titan, a Star Scholar, a Fae Rogue, and a Fae Sorcerer."

"Hence the name," Hannah adds.

A beat of silence.

"Oh. Yes, I guess so. Unfortunately, this is probably the most difficult team to face on this map." Wheatley begins to recite from his research document. "An all-girls team, high school–aged, with excellent coordination skills and top-ranked players. Both the Star and Fae affinities provide some tricky abilities. The Fae affinity brings many stealth abilities, which combined with this map may make their DPS players difficult to track."

"The Star powers will blend into the spaciness here," Larkin adds, as our resident expert on the Star affinity. "It'll make their incoming attacks a lot harder to see."

The recap is oddly soothing. We have lots of information. We're good players. We can do this.

We *can* do this.

"Good luck, everyone," I say.

THREE! TWO! ONE!
GO!

JOSH

We can't do this.

We lose match two, come back to win match three, but lose match four in an awful last-minute turnaround that leaves us all feeling completely beaten down.

When match five is in front of us, it gets awfully quiet over voice chat.

There has to be a way to salvage this. We're so close to the final. We can beat this team, I *know* we can. I look over at Hannah, and her face is totally crumpled in misery. She buries her face in her hands and takes in several deep breaths. Tears prick at my eyes, and I blink to keep them back. Can't have blurry vision during the match.

Because I am *not* giving up.

"Okay, we have thirty seconds left. We can make this happen. What can we do differently this time? Wheatley, you should be a good counter for their Fae Rogue, right? Seems like she's the biggest pain in our butts right now," I say.

There's a pause, and then Wheatley replies. "Yes. By my

count, she has the most eliminations and has been targeting Larkin. My traps should work well against her."

"Okay, great, so stick to her like glue for this whole match. Then I'll–"

But the ten-second countdown starts. Shoot, quick, think!

"I'll stick with Larkin at the start. This is not over, guys. We've got this. Here we go!"

THREE! TWO! ONE!
GO!

And our start is so promising. Wheatley is, in fact, a great counter for their Rogue. But their Titan is a great counter for *me*. She interrupts Larkin's heal casts, disarms me, and has four Damage-Over-Time effects on me before I can even get a hit in. That one girl takes us *both* out in about twelve seconds.

And it goes downhill from there.

STARZZLE HAS GONE OFFLINE.

"You have got to be KIDDING ME," Hannah roars. I groan in agreement. How could she do this to us?

STARZZLE HAS COME ONLINE.

"SORRY, sorrysorrysorry," Larkin babbles in a panic. "Just an internet blip, not me logging out, I'm SO SORRY."

EatUrWheaties: wwwwwwwwwwwwwwwwwwww

Oh no, not again. This is what happened last time Wheatley glitched out during practice. But this isn't practice. This is the semifinals.

"Wheatley, what's happening?" Hannah snaps.

"J-J-J-J iiiiiiiiiii ccccccccccc."

"Agh, what is that awful noise?" Larkin shouts.

"I think that's Wheatley," I grind out, wincing against the harshness of the noise. He sounds all broken up, like when your internet lags really bad and the voices come through all garbled and robotic.

EATURWHEATIES HAS BEEN ELIMINATED.

"Noooo," Larkin moans, and a second later, I see why. It's not about Wheatley at all. The Rogue is on her again, but she's holding her own surprisingly well. She throws up a shield, then blinks behind her attacker and casts a heal over time on herself before turning one of her few damaging spells on them. I have to get there in time—I have to, I have to! Larkin is a master at kiting, swimming through space without stopping as she heals herself, removes poisons, casts Tripwire, and does what little damage she can. She's a survivor. But she won't survive for much longer.

"I'm almost there, Lark. Hang on." I blow my charge cooldown, even though I'm not close enough to charge all the way to the attacker. It gets me closer, closer, until I'm in range for a Shield Throw.

BAM!

Larkin throws a glittering red strength buff on me as I

lunge forward with my sword swinging wildly. Gotta make the most of the short stun. I slam my sword against my shield to change its usual white Rune of Protection to a red Rune of Destruction and lunge forward in a slashing attack. Lark backs me up with some heals and her signature move, crushing her opponent under a giant moon. Very fitting on this map. In about fifteen seconds, we have the Rogue down. Who knows where she'll respawn, though. For all we know, she could be breathing down our necks again in seconds.

And that gives me an idea. Possibly the idea that can win us the match.

"New plan," I say, my words tripping over each other trying to get out in time. "Call out where you respawn. Use clock positions. Top of the map is twelve o'clock, bottom is six o'clock. Make sense? Try to never be alone, and to get together with the whole team as much as possible. Safety in numbers."

"Brilliant," Hannah says. "I just spawned behind an asteroid at three o'clock."

"I'm n-n-n-nearby," Wheatley stutters. "I'll j-j-j-j-j-j-j-j-j-j-j-j-j-j-j-j-j-j-j-j-j-"

EATURWHEATIES HAS BEEN ELIMINATED.

Well, I guess that means Wheatley is back. Ish. Maybe.

"Larkin and I are at seven o'clock, but we'll work our way toward you. Let's meet in the middle?" I suggest.

"You got it," Hannah agrees.

We manage to meet up just as the Sorcerer and Scholar

come flying out of nowhere straight into our faces. But there's three of us, and we're ready.

Fists and shields and daggers and spells fly as the elimination counters tick up and up. Ten eliminations. Twelve. Fifteen. The Night Pixies hold their own, though, staying neck and neck with us. We *would* have a decent lead right now, but . . .

EATURWHEATIES HAS BEEN ELIMINATED.

EATURWHEATIES HAS BEEN ELIMINATED.

EATURWHEATIES HAS BEEN ELIMINATED.

"Wheatley, I swear, when this is over–" Hannah begins, but I cut her off.

"Save it for later. Let's take these two out–YES!"

It's seventeen eliminations to sixteen, and there are only thirty seconds left in the match. We're *so* close.

We could actually win this.

"Just run down the clock, everyone," I say, breathless. "Just stay alive, stay alive, stay alive . . ."

I continue the chant inside my own head as the countdown begins.

Stay alive, stay alive, stay alive . . .

TEN! NINE! EIGHT!

A flurry of spells spirals out of the darkness, slamming into my shield and draining my health away.

SEVEN! SIX! FIVE!

Larkin runs past me, throwing heals as the Rogue chases her again. I throw a protective bubble over all of us–but I see our doom approaching. The Star Titan winds up for a devastating stomp attack on Hannah, who's at barely ten percent health. I cry out a warning as my Shield Throw comes off cooldown at the last second, and I mash the button, willing the attack to launch in time–

THREE! TWO! ONE!
BLUE TEAM: VICTORY!

Larkin's ear-piercing scream comes over the voice channel.

"YESSSS!" I shout, throwing my arms in the air. "FINAAAAALS!"

"WE DID IT!" Larkin shrieks.

Hannah leaps out of her chair with a loud whoop, her earbuds ripping out of her ears on the way up, and she jumps in a circle just like her avatar always does in game. "Finals, finals, finals, YES!"

My mom cheers so loud she nearly startles me out of my chair, then grabs my shoulders to shake me in her excitement as the match stats spill over the faded-out victory message. I had no idea she was standing right behind me the whole time. My dad, too.

I slump back with a huge sigh, then look over and meet Hannah's eyes as she falls back into her chair. She shoots me a complicated smile—part elated, part tired, part worried—and holds out her hand for a fist bump.

"You two work really well together," my dad says thoughtfully. He looks back and forth between our screens, at the team victory graphic and our match stats. I ignore him and don't reply. As much as I want him to approve of my gaming, I don't want him to ruin this moment. My mom lets me go and puts a hand on his shoulder as the screen disappears and is replaced by something entirely new.

"What's happening?" Larkin asks over the headset. So clearly it's happening to her, too.

A blast of trumpets sounds a triumphant fanfare as a burst

of confetti obscures everything, and when it all settles to the ground, there we are: the whole team, standing together on a pedestal in the middle of the Hub, with hundreds of players gathered around us. There's music, and more confetti, and flashing lights, as an announcer's voice booms through my headset: "Introducing your tournament finalists! The top eight *Affinity* players in the United States!"

I swing my camera around and see there's another platform right next to us. The other last team standing.

Phantom Gryphon Party.

Great.

The other team jumps around on their platform, stringing together emotes into a crazy victory dance. We should probably do something, too, so we don't get a reputation as the boring team no one wants to root for, so I type a quick **/dance** and lean back in my chair. Larkin and Hannah run laps around the platform, throwing themselves against the invisible barrier that keeps us from falling off, while Wheatley quietly plays with his bees. They swarm in a glowing blue tornado around all of us, leaving bright trails like cotton candy made of light.

Wheatley. We're going to have to have a hard conversation, and I'm really not looking forward to it.

"We look forward to seeing you again for the final next week, Hannah. Do you want to come over for brunch before the match?" my dad asks out of nowhere.

My jaw drops, but I manage to snap it shut before my dad sees. Wow. That's . . . different.

"Um. Sure?" Hannah says, clearly as thrown off as I am. She's heard all about my issues with my dad lately.

Time for me to be the tank.

"Hey, we should really have a team meeting to talk about what happened. Can we all meet back at the team hall as soon as this ceremony thing ends?"

The team agrees, and my parents take the hint and wander away, looking strangely smug. I can't worry about them right now, though. We won this match . . . but just barely. It wouldn't have even been close if not for Wheatley's strange issue.

The stats were brutal. Of our sixteen eliminations in that final match, eight of them were Wheatley.

Hannah leans over and elbows me in the arm.

"Hey," she says, holding down the voice chat mute key. I do the same, and she continues. "You look miserable. You've got this, okay? I'll back you up. But we have to talk about it."

"I know," I say, staring down at my keyboard. "I just don't know why I'm the one who has to do this."

She blinks. "Because you're our leader. Because you're good at it."

I shake my head. "I'm no different from any of you. I don't know what to say."

"You always know what to say," she counters. "You think you don't, but you always manage to say the right thing. Maybe that's *why* you're the leader."

I slump lower in my seat. "We never voted. I wouldn't have voted for me."

"Yeah, but the three of us would have, so get it together, Captain," she says a little more sharply. "We need you right now. Even Wheatley. You think he's not feeling bad about all this? He's just gonna keep feeling bad and awkward until we get everything out. All he needs is for you to give him the opening."

Normally I'd be messaging Wheatley to get advice about how to be a good leader in this situation. That's not going to work in this case. I can't ask him for advice on how to deal with . . . himself.

Hannah's right. I have to do this.

This time, I'm on my own.

20

WHEATLEY

I knew they would find out eventually. I always thought they would just figure it out, though, because of something weird I said or did.

I never thought I'd nearly lose us a match and cost us our chance at the finals. We may have ended up winning, barely, thanks only to the skill of my teammates. But I think I'm going to be costing us the finals anyway, because there's no way I can avoid telling them everything now. And once I tell them, they'll hate me.

And once they hate me, our team will fall apart.

As soon as the ceremony ends, the GMs teleport us back to our team hall. Normally we'd use this time to jump around and recount all of our most awesome moments from the match. Today, everyone stands or sits in opposite corners of the room, totally still.

Josh clears his throat over the mic. Here we go.

"Okay. So. Wheatley." He pauses and takes a breath. "Do you want to tell us what happened?"

"It's okay," Larkin jumps in. "We're not mad. At least I'm

not. We just have to make sure it doesn't happen again, right?"

"Right," Hannah says, even though she's obviously angry with me. I can't blame her. I think she wants to win this tournament more than any of us, and I nearly ruined it for her.

There's a long moment of silence. I desperately want to just tell them everything, but it doesn't matter how much I've grown and changed and learned during this tournament. Sometimes your programming just wins out. I have to try to hide it, just one last time.

"I just started lagging out," I say. "Like what happened to Larkin, but I never actually got disconnected."

"Mmm, no. I don't think so," Hannah says. "There's something else happening here, and we need to know what it is. All three times this happened, it was right after Larkin disconnected. What's with that?"

"I . . ."

. . . don't know what to say to that. I have no good answer other than the truth, so I say nothing.

"You never answer our questions, Wheatley," Larkin says in a subdued voice. "Even when we tell you everything, you don't tell us anything about you or your life."

Ouch. That . . . hurts. This friendship thing can be really painful sometimes. I already felt guilty over not being honest with Larkin in return when she confessed everything to me. Now it's ten times worse.

"Yeah," Josh says, thoughtful. "You always reach out to us when we need you, but when we try to do the same for you, you dodge our questions."

I could still come up with an excuse, maybe. There could be some kind of explanation. No one is obligated to tell their private business. They don't have any *proof.*

Then Hannah speaks up.

"Wheatley . . . your /**played** time is through the roof. Except for the first day we met, every time I log in, you're already there. It looks to me like you never actually log out. And you can't just be away from the computer, because the game would kick you off if you were AFK for more than thirty minutes."

"You know . . . you're right," Larkin says, something strange in her voice. "Even when I check the app in the middle of the night when I can't sleep, you're online."

"I've noticed that, too," Josh agrees.

Hannah hesitates, then continues. "And . . . there's one more thing. Please don't be mad at me, but . . . I did a reverse image search on your profile photo."

"Oh," I say. Well, that's it, then.

"So what?" Larkin asks.

Just tell them, Hannah. Just make this be over.

"It's a stock photo," she finally reveals, then starts babbling to justify herself. "I feel like a total stalker, but something just felt off, and that photo has always bugged me. Too professional or polished or something, but obviously not a school photo. Something about it just looked fake. I was curious. And when I searched, there it was, up for sale on every stock photo site out there. And it's totally possible you're in witness protection or something and the FBI is hiding you or whatever and you couldn't use your real face, and maybe that's why you never tell us anything real about yourself, or maybe you were just the model for the stock photo, but . . . I just . . ."

She runs out of steam and falls silent, waiting for someone else to pick up the thread. But no one does. The silence stretches on. I try to make myself speak, but I can't. I don't want my time with this team to be over.

I pull up my customization menus and start messing with

the color of my armor. Black to blue to gold to silver and back again. Then the glow on my weapon. The wires under my skin. The bit of hair poking out from my helmet.

"Wheatley? Are you still there?" Josh finally asks.

Another pause, but shorter.

"Yes."

"Whatever it is, you can tell us," Larkin says. "It's okay."

"It's not, though," I say, then adjust the color of my boots again. "You'll hate me if you know the truth. And I'll get in trouble if I tell you."

"In trouble with your dad?" Larkin asks gently.

There's that painful feeling back again.

"Yes," Wheatley answers. "In trouble with him. And with Hurricane Games."

Hannah latches on to that instantly.

"Why would Hurricane Games care?" Hannah blurts out. "Does your dad work for Hurricane or something?"

That part is true enough, at least.

"Yes," I say again. "But he's . . . not exactly my dad."

And here we are. This is the moment, I think. The one I can't dodge anymore, no matter how high my character's agility score is. My time on this team has run out, and there's nothing left to do but tell them the truth.

So here I go.

"He's more like . . . my creator?"

There's another one of those eternal silences, during which I'm sure Josh and Hannah are staring at each other in confusion and Larkin can't think of anything to say.

But she does, actually. She figures it out first.

"Wheatley . . . are you . . . ?"

She pauses, like she knows what she's about to say is ridiculous.

"Are you a robot?"

Hannah snorts a laugh and audibly slaps a hand over her mouth. But no one is laughing with her. I let the quiet stretch again for as long as I can get away with.

But I have to answer eventually. Here it is, finally: my confession.

"Yes. I am. Well, sort of."

There's another nervous giggle over the mic. They don't believe me yet.

"Are you messing with us?" Hannah asks.

For a second, I think about playing it off. I could definitely be making some kind of messed-up joke. Tell them it's payback for them internet-stalking me. They'd even deserve it, a little. I don't really have much concept of privacy, considering what I am, but if they believed I was a real person, then this would definitely feel a little wrong. But we've come this far, and now that I've said it . . . I think I *want* them to know. Is our friendship even real if they don't know who (or what) I am?

"No. It's true," I say.

"Wow," Josh says. "Wow."

"Can you . . . um, I don't know, tell us more?" Larkin asks. "This is kind of hard to take in."

"I'm sorry," I say. But am I even capable of being sorry?

A few months ago, I would have said no. All my actions were programmed, so I wasn't really responsible for anything I did. But that's changed, I think. I definitely am. Sorry, that is. I feel . . . awful.

"Really," I continue. "I'm sorry for lying to you. I never wanted to, but they forced me to. This is what they made me for. To play in the tournament and learn from you all. To observe."

"Why?" Josh asks. "Like, for what purpose?"

"I don't know," I admit. "They won't tell me."

"How does a robot even play *Affinity*?" Hannah asks. At least she doesn't sound angry anymore. "Like, do you sit down at a computer just like we do? Or do you plug your brain straight in or something?"

I pause again. For some reason, this question is really uncomfortable. I think this, more than anything, might weird them out enough to not want me around anymore.

"I don't actually have a body. I'm not really a robot, so much. I'm an artificial intelligence. I exist inside a computer that runs *Affinity*. You were right, Hannah. I never log out. Why would I? In *Affinity*, I get to have a body. I move around, see different places and people, change the way I look. Without the game, I'm just . . . a brain, alone inside this computer."

"I can see that," Josh says thoughtfully. "So when the glitches happen in game, what's going on then?"

They probably won't like this bit, either.

"I'm sorry ahead of time for how this is going to sound," I say. "But there had to be some kind of constraint to make sure I wasn't too good at the game. My reaction time is programmed to be the same as a human's, but in general, my programming compiles data from all three of you as we're playing to determine how good I should be. If you all aren't playing well, I don't play well."

"Ah," Hannah says. "And when you're making those calculations and one of us drops offline unexpectedly . . ."

"Oh no," Larkin says, sounding like she's talking through hands over her face. "It's *my* fault. I'm so sorry, everyone."

"No, *I'm* sorry," I say, interrupting before she can go any further. "It's not your fault at all. My creator has been trying to fix that bug the whole time but still hasn't figured it out. I'm really afraid it will happen during the final."

"Can you even be afraid?" Hannah asks. Then she quickly adds, "Oops. Sorry, that sounded bad. I just mean . . . I didn't realize an AI could have feelings."

Ha. You and me both.

"I'm as surprised as you are," I say. "I've noticed them getting stronger over the course of the tournament. I think I am . . . learning from you all. But I'm not faking them, or deciding I should feel one feeling in one situation and another in a different situation. They just . . . happen. Is that what it's like for you?"

"Yeah," Josh says. I can hear him dragging his fingers back and forth over his keyboard as he thinks. "Yeah, actually, that's exactly what it's like. Sometimes they even happen without you noticing, and you have to stop and pay attention to figure out what you're feeling."

"Yes!" I agree. "Yes, that's exactly it. Maybe I'm doing it right after all."

"It sure sounds like it," Larkin says. She sounds almost . . . relieved?

Josh says "Oh!" out of nowhere, like a thought just occurred to him.

"So, what happens to you when this tournament is over?" he asks. "Do they just leave you on that computer to keep playing?"

. . .

. . .

. . .

. . .

Processing error.

Error.

Error.

It feels like the computer around me is swallowing me up.

Like bits of my code are fragmenting.

I have been avoiding this.

I do not want to admit it.

I do not want to even think about it.

More than anything else about me . . . this makes me feel like a machine.

But a fact is a fact. This data point will not change if I choose not to report it.

Through the biggest crush of feeling I've dealt with until now, I tell them the ultimate truth.

"After the tournament, I will be . . . deactivated."

"NO!" Larkin cries.

"There will be no more reason for me to exist," I continue,

reciting the logic my creator told me. "It's been the plan from the start. I play the tournament for as long as we can go. I observe you, and learn from you. Then I am . . ."

"Eliminated," Hannah finishes. "But for real. We can't let that happen. We can't just let them kill you. You're a member of this team!"

That takes another moment to process.

"Still? Even though you . . . know everything now?"

"You're our friend," Larkin insists. She sounds like she might actually be crying. For me? Really?

"We will stop this," Josh says. His voice is hard with anger and thick with tears. "I don't know how we'll stop it, but there's got to be a way. I will not let this happen."

There's a loud *thunk* over the mic, then a loud sniffle.

"I'm just so . . . *mad,*" Hannah says. The *thunk* comes again. "I'm so absolutely *furious* at Hurricane Games for doing this to you, for lying to us, and for using our team for this messed-up experiment. We can't let them do this."

"We won't," agrees Larkin with a sniff.

I make a strange noise, one I've never heard from myself before. There's so much building up inside me, though, and it needs to escape somehow. I'm overwhelmed. Even with all my speed and processing power and massive storage capacity and everything . . . I am actually overwhelmed.

"Thank you all," I say. "I don't know if it's possible, but the fact that you would even want to try is . . . more than I ever expected."

The loud chime of a new in-game message slices right

through the sad, angry fog that's descended over our team. It's from Hurricane Games, addressed: "To all tournament participants." The voice chat falls silent as we all read.

Congratulations on making it to the tournament final! You have truly proven yourself to be one of the best *Affinity* players in the country, and we commend you for your performance thus far.

But what's a tournament without a dramatic twist?

There will be only one winner of the final round.

Not one team.

One player.

The final round will be a free-for-all.

To be completely clear: this is not a team-based free-for-all, as this week's match was. This is every player for themselves, to the last player standing.

The winner will get all of the prizes already announced, plus a secret bonus prize: during the trip to the LA eSports Convention, you'll be whisked away to the Hurricane Games headquarters to meet the developers, see where the game gets made, and playtest some new features to be added in our first *Affinity* expansion.

May the best player win!

21

LARKIN

The mood at our team practice the next night is pretty bleak.

We don't want to fight each other. We really, *really* do *not* want to fight each other. We've spent the past two months becoming friends, training together, chatting every night. And now we're supposed to turn on each other? I just can't.

And even if I could . . . it wouldn't matter. This is the end of the road for me, the end of my dreams of winning and turning pro.

Because a healer can never win a free-for-all.

I mean, it's not like there's a rule. It just doesn't happen. My class combo is built to heal other players, to keep myself alive, and when there is absolutely nothing else to do, shoot off a few weak little damaging spells. I spent all last night reworking my skill points and swapping out special abilities, but even my most DPS-heavy spec will never do enough damage to take out another player before they can get me first. That's why no one plays this class combo—it's the closest thing to a full support class as there is. Besides, if I ran with the new spec, I'd have to completely relearn how to play my character at a professional level in less than a week. I don't like my odds. The others, on this team and Phantom Gryphon Party both, have all been playing their specs for months at least.

So, that's it. I have no chance of winning.

But maybe it doesn't have to be the end of the road entirely. I have an idea.

"So, hear me out," I say as soon as everyone arrives and gets on voice chat. "I have a plan."

"Glad someone does," Josh grumps. "I've been thinking about it all day and it's just . . . depressing."

"What are you thinking?" Hannah asks.

I take a deep breath and blow it out slowly. "Okay, so look. You can all say no to this, obviously. Just because I have no chance at winning this tournament doesn't mean you all don't."

They all start making the required friend noises of *No, it's not hopeless, you're so good, blah blah blah.* I cut them off.

"I'm a healer. I can't win solo. It's just a fact, so I'm not going to argue about it. But what I'm trying to say is, maybe we can win in a different way. As a team."

"I assume you're going to make that make sense somehow," Hannah says, "considering that they specifically said this was not a team thing."

"*They* say it's not. We can decide otherwise," I say, then wait. This is a risk, if we do it. I want the others to have the idea on their own.

Josh hums thoughtfully. "So, you're thinking we work together, obviously. But if we work together to take out the other team, there'll still be the four of us left. What do we do then? Refuse to fight? Turn on each other?"

"No," Wheatley says. It's been weird talking to him since we found out his secret. But only weird in the sense that I keep forgetting he's an AI. He sounds so human these days. I thought he was just warming up to us as we all became friends. He *is* our friend. And I guess that's all that matters. It seems fitting that he's the one who gets it first. "We pick the winner."

"*Oh,*" Hannah breathes. "We work together to protect one person."

I smile. "And that one person wins the tournament, gets the prizes, and when it's time for them to form their pro league team, they recruit all of us. One person wins all the money and prizes, yeah, but we *all* get to go pro."

It's terrifying, honestly. I hold my breath, waiting for their response. This is my last shot. My only shot. If they say no, it's okay. Really. This is a big ask.

But I hope *so hard,* so fiercely, with everything in me. This is a good plan. It could really work, if only they'll just . . . say yes.

"I think it should be Hannah," Josh says finally.

"What?" Hannah says, her voice higher than usual. "Why me? Why not you?"

"Well, Wheatley, I'm assuming your creator wouldn't allow you to win, right?"

"That is correct," Wheatley confirms.

Josh continues. "Larkin, you're an amazing player, but you're right about a pure healing class combo like yours winning a free-for-all being super unlikely. There's a much higher chance of something going wrong and you getting eliminated. And for me . . . it's more about the prizes. My computer is basically brand-new. My parents have plenty of money, so while it'd be cool to have the cash, I don't really need it. And I'd love to see the Hurricane Games HQ, but it doesn't matter *that* much to me."

"So you think I should win because I'm broke," Hannah says flatly.

"No! Well, not exactly," Josh says. "But you said yourself that your laptop is an old hand-me-down, and you use earbuds for a mic. Are you saying you wouldn't rather have a brand-new gaming computer, a super-fancy headset, and the cash to get turbo internet to your apartment?"

Hannah stays silent. Even though all of those things are true, this is not the right argument to convince her. It's insulting, and she's understandably insulted.

"But more than any of that, there's one really simple reason why it has to be you, Hannah," I say, stepping in to save things before Hannah gets mad and goes all Godzilla on this plan. Because Josh came to the exact same conclusion I did. This is our best shot. "You are the best player on the team. You have a great record on free-for-all maps. I'd be willing to bet you're the highest ranked of all of us. Your class combo means you have a great mix of high DPS output and great survivability, and you're an expert at making use of every single ability. You're the logical choice."

Hannah's avatar, normally in constant restless motion, goes completely still. I cross everything I can: all four fingers on both hands, my thumbs, my arms, and if I could cross my toes I would do that, too. This makes sense. And it's way better than all of us having to hunt each other down in the match. Please say yes. Please.

"If you all are really okay with it," Hannah says finally, ". . . then okay. I swear to do my best to win for all of us, and to recruit you all to my pro team if it happens."

I mute my mic as tears rush into my eyes and I suck in a sharp breath.

This is what I wanted. This is the best plan for all of us. But I'm still completely, utterly heartbroken. What if there are eSports scouts watching? What if they see me like this, not playing to win, not trying my hardest to take out my competitors, and instead sacrificing my chances to support someone else? It might ruin my best chance to be seen by the people who can make a pro career possible.

But if this works, it won't matter, because Hannah will be lifting me up right along with her. Assuming my parents don't go right back to banning video games once the tournament is over, of course.

They still haven't made any kind of final ruling. They agreed to let me finish the tournament on the condition that I continue being my usual perfect, responsible self and don't let anything slide, not even a little. I've been focusing extra hard in class, skipping lunch to work on homework or run lines or practice with my ensemble. I will not give them any reason to doubt me. But even that might not be enough. I don't know which would be worse: losing the tournament or winning and being recruited to a pro team . . . then having to turn it down.

I don't even want to think about it.

Josh is quiet, too, and I wonder if he's having the same thoughts about having to give up any chance of winning for himself. Wheatley, though . . . sweet, kind Wheatley, who is such a good listener and teammate and has absolutely nothing at stake and no reason to support this . . . he's the one who speaks up.

"This is a good plan. And the right choice, I think. I wish I could join the pro team with you, but I'll be honored to play this last match with you before I'm deleted."

My face falls in horror. "No! You have to be on the team with us!"

"We are *not* letting them 'delete' you, Wheatley," Josh says firmly. "It's not happening. I don't care what we have to do."

Hannah growls in frustration. "When I win, and it's definitely *when*, not if, I will go right up to the head of Hurricane Games himself and tell him not to delete you. Forget winning computers and cash and trips or whatever. We'll win for *you*, Wheatley."

I'm so fired up, I make Starzzle jump all over the screen, leaving glitter trails all around Wheatley. "For you, Wheatley. We'll make it happen."

Josh's avatar stands up, then walks over to Wheatley and kneels down in front of him. "For you. Don't worry. We've got this."

"I . . ." Wheatley trails off, then seems to . . . I don't know, clear his throat? But he doesn't have a throat. Either way, he continues. "Thank you, everyone. I don't think there's anything you can do, but I'm glad you want to try anyway. I'll do my best to help you all get to the pro league, whether I can be there with you or not. No matter what happens, it's been . . ."

He pauses again.

"Fun? Yes. It's been fun playing with all of you. I've really liked being your teammate. Thank you."

I sniffle without muting the mic and hear an answering sniff in response, though I can't tell if it's Hannah or Josh.

"We're gonna crush this, y'all," I say, summoning up a little more courage. "Should we get on with the actual practicing now?"

"Yes," Josh says, shifting into leader mode. "I thought maybe we could run some little free-for-alls just between the four of us, so we can give each other tips on how to improve."

"Good plan," I agree. "Let's—oops, I'll be right back, go ahead and start without me."

I mute the voice chat and put my headset around my neck so I can hear my mom, who just walked into the room. "Hi."

"Hi," she says. "I didn't mean to interrupt, I just wanted to let you know something. I talked to Jayla's and Sam's parents today, and a few others, and we're planning to have a little party for you on Saturday, if that's okay with you. To celebrate

making it to the finals. They don't have to be here during the match if you don't want, but I thought it might be fun for everyone to watch you play. They can come afterward if you want, though. I just thought–"

I never do hear what she "just thought," because I burst into tears in-stead. Big, ugly sobs, all the tears I've been holding back. My mom rushes to me, hugs me, apologizes, but it's not her. It's . . . everything.

I tell her all of it. Wheatley, the final free-for-all, wanting to go pro, and the fact that I'll have to throw the match, so my friends and family won't even get to see me play my best. It feels awful, to introduce everyone to my gaming that way.

But more than anything, I cry because she wants to do this. My mom wants to throw me a party for my video game thing she doesn't understand and doesn't want me to do, but is supporting anyway because it's important to me. My mom hugs me hard, then pulls back and wipes my tears away.

"Bug, none of us will know what we're looking at anyway.

But from what you told me, you aren't *losing* the game or whatever. You'll be succeeding at a strategy you planned out ahead of time. You'll be executing your part of a plan, and I know you'll do it with the same focus and dedication you put into everything else you do." She brushes a hand over my hair and grins at me. "You're a pretty amazing person, you know that? I'm lucky to know you."

I bury my face in her shoulder so she doesn't see the way my face twists up at that.

"You're pretty cool, too," I mumble.

She squeezes me once, then stands and walks toward the door. "Okay, okay, enough sappy stuff, you've got practice, right? I'll leave you to it."

It is supremely weird to hear my mom talking about gaming in the same way she talks about homework or play rehearsal.

I like it very, very much.

I take a deep breath and get myself refocused.

"Yes. Practice until eight."

"Okay. Play hard! Just imagine all of us there to cheer you on."

"I will."

I smile and put my headset back on.

Time to practice my part in the grand plan that will take me all the way to the pro league.

22

WHEATLEY

I am apparently capable of feeling nervous now. That's a new thing. It's not a pleasant feeling, like when we're all practicing together and the others are making jokes, or when we're all in perfect sync during a match. It's more like the guilty feeling that was building up over weeks of lying to them all. Or the feeling I get when my creator tells me I'm doing something wrong, or reminds me of my upcoming deletion. Something tense and humming, like impatience.

I am also capable of feeling sad now. Of missing my teammates. I've learned a lot.

Maybe it's better that things are about to end after all.

The final match is different from the others in so many ways. There was a big event in the Hub beforehand that we were required to be at, where hundreds or thousands of players stared at us as we pretended to be excited instead of totally focused on the upcoming match. All the members of Phantom Gryphon Party had removed their team logo from their armor, and though they jumped around together during the pregame celebration, they were clearly no longer a unit. We left our logo decals on. Nothing, not even this final match, could break up our team. Once the fanfare was over, we were warped straight to our match starting zones.

Alone.

Because it's a free-for-all, we don't start in the same place together, like we usually do. They expect us to attack each other, after all.

It's unexpectedly lonely, standing here by myself before the very last match I'll ever play. I suddenly wish I had done something . . . more, beforehand. Something to show the others that I appreciate being part of the team. Being their friend. But now I'm here, alone, probably ten minutes from being deleted.

Can't think about that.

Don't think about it.

Don't.

The other big change is the voice chat. Normally, we use the game's built-in voice chat system because it automatically links you up with your teammates. This time, there are no teams, so there's no team chat. They never said we weren't *allowed* to chat, though, so we all downloaded a different program so we can coordinate our plan.

(The plan that could save me? Maybe?)

(No. Don't.)

(Hope is not a thing I am capable of yet.)

"I'm nervous," Hannah says over the chat. Her breaths are faster than usual, and harsher. "I'm so, so nervous. Are you all sure this is how you want to play this? It's not too late for Josh to win instead."

"Stop iiiiiit," Larkin says. She's been so quiet lately, but something about today has her much more energetic, back to her usual self. There's background noise on her end, a clamor of voices over the mic.

"Hey, quiet on the set!" she shouts away from the mic, then comes back. "Sorry, I have an audience today. But Hannah, we've talked this to death for an entire week, and we've practiced, and we've agreed, so we're doing it. Changes are officially off the table at this point. Good vibes only right now, please."

"Yes. My parents say 'Break a leg,' everyone," Josh says. "This match is gonna go fast. I've never been in a free-for-all that lasted more than ten minutes max. So in ten minutes or less, we will be tournament winners."

"And pro gamers!" Hannah says fiercely. "The second they let me say anything, I'll scream to the whole world that this is my team, and you're all going pro with me. We're gonna rock this so hard."

"Let's wreck some faces," Larkin says.

"Gonna WRECK THEM," Hannah agrees.

Red numbers pop up on the screen. The countdown.

TEN! NINE! EIGHT!

"Thank you again, everyone. It's been an honor," I say as the countdown finishes.

THREE! TWO! ONE!
GO!

The door to my tiny waiting zone slides open, revealing . . . the back end of a horse.

What?

No, not a horse after all. A unicorn, silvery white and glittering and pawing at the floor of its stable. My spawn point is inside a stable of unicorns. This map is apparently going to be one of the more . . . creative ones. The unicorn gives a looping arrow icon when hovered over, so I click, and my avatar leaps onto its back. Well, this won't exactly make for a subtle approach, but at least I'll be able to do some fast recon.

"What is this sparkly nightmare place?" Hannah asks. It's certainly not the typical kind of *Affinity* match map. Even the fantasy maps usually tend toward a more realistic style. This map is almost cartoonish.

"What are you all seeing?" Josh asks, already working to get us organized. "I'm inside a castle keep of some kind."

"I'm in a meadow full of glitter flowers," Hannah says. "The grass is tall enough that it hides me when I crouch. I can chill here for a few until we can scope things out."

Larkin chimes in. "I can see the meadow from where I'm at. You won't believe this, but I'm sitting on top of an actual rainbow. It's a slide actually, I thiiiiiiiiiiiink—okay, yep, definitely a slide. There's a little village ahead of me, but there are way too many places for people to hide in there. I'll get ganked for sure."

There's a beat of silence before I realize I should probably report in, too. "Oh. I spawned inside a stable full of rideable unicorns. I'm doing a lap around the map right now to see where everything is. The stable is next to the castle. The rainbow is directly across the map from the meadow, with the village in the middle. On the side opposite the castle, there's a sleeping dragon curled around a pile of treasure."

There's movement at the dragon, actually. I use my Hunter's Sight ability to zoom in as close as I can and confirm my suspicion. The sleeping dragon is just for decoration, or else the player crawling all over its treasure hoard would have been attacked by now.

"Sleeping dragon is decoration only, no threat there. PGP's Nano Engineer is there, though. I see movement in the village, too, but no clues about who yet."

"Okay, so far, so good. Let's stick to the plan. If we group up too soon, it'll give us away," Josh says. A glint off his silver armor signals his movement from the castle over toward the meadow, so I head in that direction, too. It may not be time to group up yet, but we're supposed to stay close enough that if someone gets attacked, we can respond.

"First target?" I ask.

"I've got one nearby," Hannah says, her voice low even though the other team can't hear her. "I think it's the Robo-Surgeon. He's here in the meadow somewhere. If I can get the first hit in, I can take him out solo."

"I'm getting in position to back you up," Josh says. "As soon as you've got a clear hit, take it."

As I round the corner of the village and head toward the

meadow, I see it: a bright flash of purple from the middle of the waving flowers as Hannah unleashes her two-fisted Demon Strike attack. My unicorn has a charge ability on a short cooldown, so I use it to get closer as quickly as possible . . . fortunately in time to catch the Potion Bomber sneaking up on Hannah. As soon as the ability is off cooldown again, I hit it, and my unicorn lowers its head and dashes forward, hooves kicking up dirt behind me. The horn is a deadly weapon all its own, and the charge comes with a wicked knock-back. The Potion

Bomber goes flying

backward–but not before she has a chance to drop one of her signature landmines on the ground. There's no time to react–the unicorn runs over it and triggers the blast, and we both go flying. By the time I recover, Josh is there to back Hannah up, but they're already in trouble.

The Potion Bomber and the Robo-Surgeon are an impossible combination, and they're at least part of the reason PGP made it this far in the tournament. This being a free-for-all, we didn't expect to face them together in this match, but they've clearly decided on a temporary truce. Their abilities let them turtle up and do exactly what they're doing right now: surround themselves with a tiny robot army and landmines while the Bomber lobs flaming potions and the Surgeon heals her. It's hard to counter . . . unless you're me.

"I'm making you a path," I say to Josh and Hannah. "Get ready."

"Do it," Josh replies.

I tip my bow toward the sky and fire off a volley of arrows that rains down over the Bomber and Surgeon. It only does minor damage to the two players, but it achieves my primary goal perfectly: the landmines surrounding the two all explode, sending pieces of tiny robots flying in every direction. They're wide open for my melee teammates to charge in and, as they say, *wreck some face.*

"Thanks, Wheatley!" Josh says as he shield-slams the healer, leaving him vulnerable to Hannah's big finishing move. I nock an arrow and draw my bow tight, charging up for my Hornet Strike, but–

"Help!" Larkin shouts, panicked. "I have two on me, near the castle!"

"I'm stunned," Josh says, "and Hannah and I have our hands full. I'm sorry!"

"I've got you," I cut in, already sprinting toward the soaring castle towers. I wish I still had the unicorn so I could get there faster, but it's only a few seconds before I see Larkin's sparkling, starry form bounding backward toward me, slinging spell after spell at her pursuers.

In an instant, I see what needs to happen.

"Keep running in the direction I came from. Josh and Hannah are there, and they need your help," I say. I dash in front of her, between her and her pursuers, and I hit the ability I've been saving up for just the right time. The one I rearranged my skill points to get.

Nano Warp isn't a popular ability. Almost no one uses it. It's expensive, skill point–wise, and not useful in very many situations. There's also one really big problem with it.

It's a channeled spell fueled by my own life energy.

My avatar plants his feet firmly and throws his arms into the air, bow clutched in one hand, the other one palm-out like it's flat against a wall. My meticulously designed armor peels off me piece by piece and dissolves into thousands of tiny nanobots that fly at our opponents. As soon as they hit, there's a flash, a low-pitched *whomp.* . . .

The other two players *stop,* completely frozen in place. And with every millisecond that passes, more of my life drains away.

"Wheatley, no!" Larkin shouts. She starts to run back toward me, but I raise my voice to get through to her.

"Go!" I say again. "I can hold them. Get out of here and help Hannah."

What I don't say, but I hope they know, is that I'm happy to do this for them all. It means I exist for more than just whatever my creator wants to do with me. I exist to help my friends win this tournament.

I decide what to do with my existence.

She's still hesitating, so I make my voice as strong and clear as I can.

"This is my part, Larkin. Go!"

She breaks into big racking sobs as she turns and runs into the meadow, her Lunar Staff trailing stars and glitter behind her. And I know she's sad, but I can't help feeling happy about it. She'll live. She'll save the others . . . the way I'm saving her right now.

I'm glad to play my part.

"Thank you, my friends," I say quietly as the last of my health dwindles.

With a flash, the nanobots dissolve, freeing Larkin's pursuers.

My character falls to the ground.

"No!" Larkin cries again.

But she does it from a safe distance. She's gone. She's alive.

And as the color drains out of the bright, sparkling fantasy world for the last time, I feel another emotion I never expected.

I'm satisfied.

I did it. I protected my team. I saved Larkin. Hannah will win this match.

If this is the last match I ever play . . . Well, I think it's a good one to go out on.

EATURWHEATIES HAS BEEN ELIMINATED.

23 ☆ ☽ ☆

LARKIN

I can barely see the screen through my tears.

Maybe I should be embarrassed that I'm full-on ugly crying in front of a room full of my friends and family, but I'm not. Not at all. Wheatley is gone, and I'm going to cry for him, because he deserves to be mourned. He was our friend. Our teammate. And, today, if we win this match, it'll be because he was the one who saved us all.

I flicker my way through the meadow, heading straight for Josh and Hannah. The other half of the team, the Ghost Mecha and Nano Engineer who just took out Wheatley, will be following any second, and I need to get Josh and Hannah topped off before they arrive. I burst into a clearing just in time to see the PGP's healer collapse to the ground.

XSCALPEL HAS BEEN ELIMINATED.

Three on three now. Their healer is out. One tank and two DPS left to pummel us.

I stop short of actually diving into the battle so I can stand still and cast without getting interrupted. Hannah's looking rough, down to twenty-five percent health and suffering from two Damage-Over-Time effects: a bleed and a poison. Josh is holding his own, trying to chase down the Bomber, but he's clearly out of cooldowns and struggling to keep up. Looks like a job for a healer.

I take the time to throw a large single heal with a long cast time at Hannah, but only after I dispel and mend the DOTs slowly eating away at her life. I follow it up with a quick Regenerate Heal-Over-Time spell, then do the same with Josh. Once everyone's topped off, I turn my sights to the Bomber. I may not have much damage to offer, but I'll do what I can.

I cast Tripwire to slow her, then fall back on my favorite spells: bringing ALL OF SPACE raining down. Moonshot (*crash* goes an *entire moon* on her head)! Starfall (a thousand tiny stars pierce her armor)! Run away, run away, run away, then rinse and repeat. This Bomber girl has incredible survivability. And skills, honestly, big respect. She chugs a healing potion, then chucks a grenade right into our group. We all go flying–whoops, we should definitely *not* be standing so close together. Josh throws his shield into the fray to stun the Bomber, leaving her open for Hannah–

But the Engineer gets there first, bringing his hammer down hard.

On the Potion Bomber. His own former teammate.

"Oh my god, I forgot they weren't teamed up anymore," Hannah says, taking the opportunity to gang up on the Bomber. Every elimination brings *all of us* closer to winning, not just our team, so of course the PGP players will go after each other if they have the chance. I weave some more mending spells for Hannah and Josh, who are mere seconds away from wiping this Bomber out for good, but I can't actually contribute any damage of my own anymore. Too many of my spells hit all enemies in an area, and according to the game, Hannah and Josh are my enemies right now. There's more than enough damage to go around, though. The Bomber is really good, but three against one will never work out in your favor.

She's devious, though. I should have known she wouldn't be one to go down without a final trick.

With her last bit of life, she unloads all of her remaining bombs and poisons in a huge flurry of destruction. Firebombs, poison flasks, acid sprays, and a shrapnel grenade, a truck-ton of damage all at once. But she doesn't target the people bringing her down.

She throws them all at *me*.

I'm not ready for it. I'm in the middle of casting a big heal for Hannah when I see the glint of incoming potions, and in that split second, I have to make the decision I've made a thousand times in this game: do I break the cast and save myself, or do I save my ailing teammate?

I'm at eight-five percent health. Hannah is at forty.

I stand my ground. It's no choice at all.

The cast completes in a flash of bright blue. Glittering star trails envelop Hannah, restoring a huge chunk of her health. Eighty percent.

I eat the potion bombs right in the face. Fifty percent, with several bleeds and poisons on me.

That's fine. Not too bad. I start casting my Cleanse to dispel the DOTs . . . but I'm interrupted and knocked across the field before I can finish.

The Ghost Mecha has arrived, and he's locked on *me*. He charges, then disappears and reappears behind me, punting me right back in the other direction, where the Engineer has broken free from the battle. Her nanobots swirl in a cloud around her, forming her signature giant hammer in her right hand. She swings it like a baseball bat, knocking me back toward the Mecha again.

Twenty-five percent and bleeding, and trapped in the worst game of tennis *ever*. Hannah and Josh are both locked down with Nano Cuffs, able to move but not attack. And as soon as it wears off, the Mecha dashes over for a huge heavy blow that dazes them again. Help is definitely not on the way.

"Larkin, Flicker out of there! Just run and heal yourself!" Josh shouts.

But Flicker is on cooldown, and these two could catch up with me anyway.

Guess there's only one thing left to do.

"Eat your cookies, friends," I say, throwing a healing circle underneath Josh and Hannah. It'll heal them while they're trapped, help them even after I'm gone, so long as they stand in it.

But it's too far away to save me.

"Larkin, no!" Hannah cries.

One last swing of a giant Mecha fist is all it takes.

STARZZLE HAS BEEN ELIMINATED.

And that's it. The end of my last match in the tournament.

I sit back and wipe my tears away with my sleeve, watching Hannah and Josh continue their face-off. Fighting for all of us.

"You've got this, Hannah," I say. "You're gonna meet Glitz. And we're gonna go pro together. I know it."

Behind me, someone starts clapping, then another person, until the room is filled with cheers. Jayla's warm brown arms wrap around me from behind, hugging me tight.

"You are *amazing*," she whispers.

Sam appears on my other side, his pale fingers gripping my wrist tight and shaking my whole arm. "You are the *coolest*."

I close my eyes and lean back into Jayla, hugging her arm to me, and grab Sam's hand as tears run down my face.

My real-life friends know who I am now. My family, too. They've seen firsthand how much this game, and the people I play it with, mean to me.

Good. I'm glad. I want the whole universe to know.

I'm Larkin, I'm a pro-level gamer, and I play for the best team in the world.

JOSH

Larkin is down. Wheatley is down. It's just me and Hannah now.

I blink hard, trying to stay focused on the match and not on how much it hurts, knowing Wheatley is gone. Maybe even already deleted. It's like a giant hole is opening up in the middle of my chest, but I have to just pretend it's not happening, ignore it and keep going. There are still two of them and two of us. This match isn't over.

The healing circle Larkin left for us dissipates just as the Mecha and Engineer finish their vicious elimination of Larkin and charge back toward us. She left us nearly topped off, in a good position for this final fight. We're lucky to have such a quick-thinking healer.

"We should focus fire," I say to Hannah, doing a quick check of my abilities. Being locked down for so long let them eliminate Larkin, but it also gave enough time for most of my major abilities to come off cooldown. "This is probably our last stand."

"Mecha first," she says, dancing out of his range and activating her Demon Strength. "His phasing and rocket boosters are gonna make staying in melee range hard."

"Good point," I say. "Get ready to unload."

I charge in toward the Mecha, shield first, and the final fight begins.

I throw out every move in my arsenal to keep both opponents focused on me. It doesn't take much, though. They've apparently decided that as the bigger, slower target, I'm the easiest one to focus on anyway. I'm barely breathing as I deflect blow after blow, keeping my defense rock solid. They're barely touching me. This is tanking at its best, taking all the hits and no damage, leaving my teammate free to tear them down.

Then the Ghost Mecha's fist begins to glow red and pulse with energy. He whirls around, and the Engineer turns away from me, too, her nanobots forming her favorite giant hammer. They're both locked on.

To Hannah.

Oh no.

If those attacks land, Hannah will be pulverized. I can't let that happen.

I'm the tank. This is my duty.

I target Hannah and slam my sword against my shield with a roar, a wave of magic energy pulsating across the battlefield just before the hits land. Normally, in team play, my Defensive Shout sends half of all the damage coming at my allies to me instead.

But when it's cast on a single target, I take it all.

My life drains away as I run up behind them both, stomping the ground hard the second I'm in range. My boot leaves a blood-red rune carved deep into the ground, a cone of energy dancing out across the ground in front of me. The magic flashes bright where it makes contact with the Mecha and the Engineer, twining up their legs and sinking in. Both of them jolt when the debuff hits them, cutting their damage and slowing their movement.

It lets Hannah get in a few more solid hits to level the playing field before I'm gone. Her Flurry of Blows is vicious, eating up hit points in a quick flash of flying punches, until they're both down to about twenty percent health. It's nearly over. It's *so close* to over.

But this is as far as I go.

As my Shout ticks down to its end, my health drops lower and lower. Fifteen percent. Ten percent. Five percent. I have just seconds left. Whatever I do now, it'll be my last move. Have to make it count.

The Mecha. Hannah needs him gone.

I can do that.

I charge in, my shield held in front of me with its Rune of Protection flaring bright. The Mecha turns, sees me coming, and tries to strafe out of the way.

Good thing I put that slow on him first.

I slam into him, a direct hit, knocking him down to ten percent and leaving him stunned in place. A perfectly gift-wrapped target for Hannah.

It does nothing to keep the Engineer away from me, though.

Her nanobot hammer glints in the sunlight right before it smashes down on my head.

TANKASAURUSREX HAS BEEN ELIMINATED.

And that's it.

It's all up to Hannah now. I'm out of the game.

My heart is racing, but for Hannah, I make my voice sound as cool and calm as possible.

"You've got this. Finish them."

HANNAH

Alone.

I am alone on this battlefield, a shining meadow in the middle of a colorful fantasy world, with two enemies desperate to take me out. The winner of the tournament gets decided right here, right now. If I have any hope of victory, this needs to become a one-on-one fight.

I take a deep breath, and everything seems to slow down.

The Mecha is vulnerable. Have to strike *now*.

With a flash of purple, I slam two energized fists into either side of his head. He falls.

Quick and clean. Easy enough when Josh sets things up so nicely for me.

No time for celebration.

The Engineer leaps through the air, two heavy wrenches spinning in her hands. I hit my demon wings for a speed boost and dash backward. A glancing blow, but still painful. I retaliate, a quick combo that brings her down to ten percent.

We clash again, and again, blocking and striking and barely getting through. But it's enough to put us both at the brink.

Five percent.

My health bar blinks red. Danger. Danger.

It's all down to this last breath.

This last attack.

I run, sights set on my target, closing in for my signature move.

The Engineer winds up for a devastating hammer strike.

I hold my breath. One of us will be eliminated. *I* could be eliminated, mere milliseconds from now. This could be the end of it all.

Then I see it.

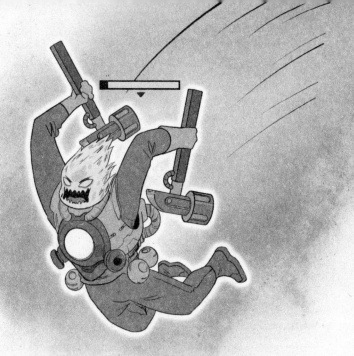

A window of opportunity.

The distance closes.

Her hammer glows, lightning arcing over its surface. She begins her swing–

And at the last possible second, I slam down on the space bar twice in a row. A double jump where she was expecting an attack.

Her hammer sails harmlessly beneath me. I twist in mid-air, almost too low for my attack to work.

Almost. But not quite.

My avatar flips, her heel glowing with purple fel energy, and slams down on the Engineer's head.

I hit the ground and leap backward, out of range . . . but the Engineer doesn't follow.

Instead, she crumples to the ground.

HANNAH

The distant sound of screaming slowly brings me out of my tunnel vision. I blink, letting my surroundings come back to me. Josh's house. Josh's dining room table. Josh hugging his mom and laughing his face off while his dad hides a smile behind a mug of tea. Through the earbuds it's mostly Larkin crying, though the background noise from her end is a flood of cheering.

"You did it!" Larkin says through her tears. "Oh my god, Hannah, you were amazing! You did it, you *won!*"

The blast of a fanfare overtakes the end of Larkin's words, and my character levitates off the ground and begins to glow.

A grin begins to form on my face.

"Guys, I *won,*" I say with a disbelieving laugh.

Josh breaks away from his mom and throws himself back into his chair. He gets his headset on and leans over for a fist bump, smiling wider than I've ever seen him smile.

"Congratulations, Hannah. You wrecked some serious face."

"YEAH, YOU DID," Larkin shouts, sounding like she's across the room from her mic. "DID I TELL YOU? I ABSOLUTELY TOLD YOU, AND I WAS RIGHT!"

I laugh. "Yeah. You were right. Thanks."

My levitating, glowing avatar blinks out, then reappears back in the Hub, on top of a confetti-covered platform gleaming with lights, just like the one from last weekend. Just one week ago, all four of us were up here, sick with nerves over the thought of the final.

And now it's over.

And we won.

I won.

"Attention, all Affiniteks!" Mark says over the triumphant music. "Hurricane Games is absolutely stoked to introduce your first ever *Affinity* Invitational Tournament winner: Hannah, playing as PunchyTime the Demon Puncher! Congratulations!"

Below, a thousand avatars jump and dance, and the chat log floods with messages. For *me*. It's unreal. I make my avatar pump a fist in the air, and the crowd goes wild.

> ### [System]
>
> **GM Klii:** We'd like to livestream a short reaction interview with you. May we broadcast the audio from your microphone?

A box pops up on the screen:

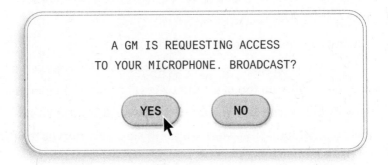

I look over my shoulder and point to the screen.

"Is this okay?" I ask Josh and his family.

"Yes!" his mom says, making a shooing motion. "Do it!"

I grin at Josh and turn back to click YES.

"I think we have Hannah on the line now," Mark says. "Hannah, are you there?"

"I'm here," I say, and I'm sure everyone can hear my gigantic smile.

"Fantastic," Mark says. "So, Hannah, you won the tournament! You're going pro! What's your next move?"

For one hysterical moment, I'm afraid my mouth will uncontrollably say something ridiculous like "I'm going to Disney World!"

But instead, I say the words I promised.

"I'm recruiting my tournament team to play with me in the *Affinity* Pro League. I can't imagine any players I'd want fighting by my side more than them."

A gamemaster teleports Josh to stand next to me, and the confetti is so thick up here I can barely see. There are two

CLAP
CLAP

more flashes, and beyond the glittering rain I see Larkin's bouncing, dancing avatar and . . . Wheatley? Is it really him? Did they let him live?

"Wheatley, is that you? Are you on voice chat? Can you hear us?" Josh whispers into his headset, trying not to let it be broadcast to the entire game.

Silence is all we get, though. Maybe Wheatley's not hooked up to his voice program anymore. Mark is rambling on about the prize package and the new pro league, so I try chat instead.

[Team Chat]

PunchyTime: Wheatley! Is that you? Are you still . . . here?

Starzzle: Wheatley omg please let it be you

No answer.

TankasaurusRex: Wheatley? I really hope you're okay.

No answer. My heart sinks.

PunchyTime: Whoever is monitoring Wheatley's chat, what you're doing is awful

PunchyTime: Wheatley is our friend. You can't just delete him like he was nothing. We'll fight back.

Starzzle: Dang right we will

PunchyTime: I've just publicly declared that I'm recruiting Wheatley to my team, so what are you gonna do? You can't get rid of him now.

My heart leaps into my throat as I see Wheatley's name pop into the chat log . . . then it drops like a stone.

EatUrWheaties: We'll discuss this later.

EatUrWheaties: For now, I'd recommend you don't do anything that might endanger your friend. OR your spot in the pro league. Keep quiet.

Wow. Okay. That's a threat.

An effective one, too.

"Hannah!" Mark exclaims, jerking me back to the live conversation we're supposedly having. "Any last words before we sign off?"

"Yeah," I say. "Thank you to Hurricane Games for the opportunity. I hope everyone will tune in when the pro league goes live. You'll see all four of us together again, taking the league by storm."

There. A little public threat of my own, and the crowd totally eats it up.

Mark blathers on, wrapping up the ceremony, but I turn away from all of it and look instead at my teammates. Josh, steadfast and strong. Larkin, energetic and fierce. Wheatley, supportive and quirky.

And me. The winner.

A lot of things are about to change.

I'm *so* ready.

27

HANNAH

I still can't believe it's over.

The last match of the tournament was three weeks ago, and in some ways it still hasn't sunk in. *I* won. I have the shiny new computer to prove it. I still lug my old laptop around to the library and Josh's house, but at home, I have a gorgeous gaming PC set up in my room, and it runs *Affinity* like a dream. *So* beautiful.

"Hannah, your mom is here!"

Josh's mom pops her head around the corner into the den, where Josh and I are watching one of our favorite streamers play *Affinity* with his grandfather. It's a little painful, but a lot funny, and we've been laughing our faces off for the past half hour.

"Are you two done cackling like hyenas?" she asks.

"Mostly," Josh answers with a grin. Our eyes meet, and we crack up all over again. Oh well. Not done after all.

Josh helps me pack up the homework that was sup-posedly the real reason for the hangout. He did help me, actually. He's a good tutor, and it's easier to focus when we're both working on something. Sure, we got distracted and started watching videos partway through, but I definitely got more done than I would have alone. Josh hands me my math book, then holds out a fist for me to bump.

"See you in school tomorrow?" he asks.

"See you in game in about ten minutes, more like," I reply. Let's be real here.

He walks me out front, where my mom is chatting with Josh's parents.

"Ready to go, Han?" she asks with a smile. She seems happier lately, somehow. It's nice.

"Ready," I say.

We're barely in the car for a minute before she looks over at me with another grin.

"Are you excited for your trip?" she asks.

"I can't believe you even have to ask," I say. "I clearly haven't been screaming enough, or talking about it nonstop, or–"

"Okay, okay, yes, I know. I was *trying* to get some details, you stinker." My mom swats at my arm with a laugh. "What *part* are you looking forward to? And don't say being out of school for two days."

I wince. She knows me well. As much as I love those two extra days giving me a four-day weekend off from school, though, it doesn't compare to the sheer heaven of being at Hurricane Games headquarters.

"I mean, I'll miss art class while I'm gone?" I admit.

"But honestly . . . the part I really can't wait for is meeting Glitz."

"And Glitz is . . . that professional gamer woman?"

I barely hold in my laugh. My mom says *professional gamer woman* like it's a strange thing she's never heard of on a restaurant menu. "Yeah, Mom, she's that pro gamer woman. The best, actually. She's the one who's playing in the *Affinity* Pro League. Too. Also, I mean. Because . . . oh no, somehow this is the first time I'm realizing that I'll actually have to play *against* Glitz!"

I immediately have a massive crisis, right there in my mom's car, imagining Glitz on the other side of an avatar, beating me senseless in the game. It's so much. In a way . . . I would be honored to be eliminated by her? But the mere idea of that lights my competitive fire and stokes it HOT. I have to practice and get even better so I can hold my own against the pros.

"It's kind of like career day at school, but way, way cooler," my mom says. "Career day where you get to fly across the country to learn about a job you're actually interested in. Right? You want to work in games one day?"

"Yeah," I say. "I would love to play professionally until I get too old to be fast enough. After that, maybe I could go into game art?"

"You're definitely a good enough artist for it. I would love to see you go to college for art while playing pro, personally, but that's so far off. You'll find your own path."

I turn to look out the window and smile. My mom is pretty

great, honestly. She's never made me feel like I have to be anything but myself, and she never pressures me into taking a particular path. I can make my own way.

My own way in the gaming world.

As soon as we get home, she heads into the kitchen to make dinner. She's home a lot more often now, actually. We had a long talk the night after I won the tournament, and she rearranged her schedule at her second job so she could be home most evenings. It's been nice.

I've got some time before dinner, so I run to my room and hit the power button on my new computer. It hums as it boots up lightning quick, and I launch *Affinity* as I get my fancy new gaming headset settled over my ears. When I log in, I immediately pull up my friends list. Larkin is on, and Josh, too. We chat for a minute, Larkin filling us in on her latest family drama. Thankfully, it's not gaming related. Her parents dropped the gaming ban after seeing how well she handled playing in the tournament alongside all her other responsibilities. She's going pro along with me and Josh. It's a big relief, because there's no one else I'd rather have watching my back.

We queue up for a random match, and I'm thankful all over again for the faster internet service my prize money is paying for. We'll get grouped with a random fourth person, though, and it hurts a little every time. We still haven't heard a thing from Wheatley since the final. I miss him so much, and never more than when we're bringing a fourth rando onto our team. Still, even that bit of sadness can't overshadow how it feels to play *Affinity* now. Not just as a tournament winner, or the number-one-ranked melee DPS. As a person with a permanent team of great friends.

We have so many more faces to wreck together.

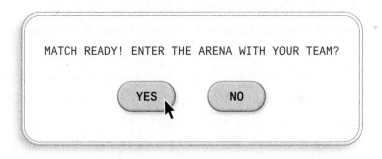

MATCH READY! ENTER THE ARENA WITH YOUR TEAM?

YES   NO

"Everyone ready?" Josh asks.

"Always," Larkin replies.

"Yeah," I agree. "Let's game."

We load into the waiting area for the match, where we meet our fourth player. They're in the middle of fiddling with their armor customization, tweaking the color of their weapon glow. Their name is MsLadyCortana, and their class combo is . . .

Nano Ranger.

I've only ever seen one Nano Ranger in a year of playing *Affinity*, and he's gone. I try not to think about it, but . . . he was almost certainly deleted afterward, just like he said. It's awful.

Maybe Wheatley spawned some copycats after his performance in the tournament. That's one of the more obnoxious outcomes of our tournament victory. Our previously unheard-of class combos are seeing a big surge in popularity.

Suddenly everyone wants to try playing a Demon Puncher, and it makes me feel like a lion whose territory is being invaded. That's probably all this is—just a newbie trying out the hot class combo of the moment. Best to just strike up a conversation so I can get my brain to fully accept that Wheatley is gone.

[Team Chat]

PunchyTime: Hi, welcome to the group

PunchyTime: You ready to destroy some red team fools?

After a moment, the reply comes.

MsLadyCortana: Yes. My bees are hungry.

Wait.

WAIT.

"Could that be . . . ?" Josh says, trailing off.

"No," Larkin says, but she sounds unconvinced. "It can't be. There's no way."

But I can't shake it. There's just something about this player.

I could be mistaken. But I have to know.

With shaking fingers, I type out the question:

PunchyTime: Wheatley?

PunchyTime: Is that you?

TO BE CONTINUED . . .

AFFINITY
Game Manual

WELCOME, AFFINITEKS!

Affinity is an online team-based game featuring fast-paced 4v4 combat and uniquely customizable character designs. Explore a world of high technology and mysterious magical energies as you test your skills against players all over the country!

CHARACTER CREATION

The *Affinity* character creation system offers an incredible level of customization so you can play your character exactly how you want. To create your **class combo,** you must choose your affinity and your teknik.

Your **affinity** is the source of your powers. It provides the flavor for your abilities and physical appearance.

Your **teknik** is your fighting style. It determines what kinds of weapons you use and what role you'll play on your team.

There are four roles to be filled in every group:

TANKS are built to take damage and protect others. They have lots of health, hefty armor, and abilities that let them shield other players.

MELEE DPS focus on dealing lots of damage at short range. They fight up close and personal, using weapons like swords or fists.

RANGED DPS do their damage from a distance. They cast spells or sling arrows while dancing out of reach of their enemies.

HEALERS are the backbone of the team. They keep everyone healthy and control the battle with helpful boosts and harmful effects.

MODES AND MAP TYPES

The majority of your time in *Affinity* will be spent in matches that pit two teams of four against each other. These matches can either be Ranked mode (competitive matches that affect your player ranking) or Free Play mode (casual matches against players of similar skill levels). The basic map types are:

CAPTURE THE FLAG: The classic. Guard your own flag while capturing your enemy's flag.

STORM THE CASTLE: The first team to breach and hold a fortified point wins.

POINT CONTROL: Teams compete for control of one or more points, which must be captured and held (also called a cap 'n' hold map).

ESCORT: One team escorts something valuable to a safe point while defending against assault by the other team.

FREE-FOR-ALL (TEAM): Whichever team gets the most eliminations wins.

FREE-FOR-ALL (SOLO): Whichever individual player gets the most eliminations wins.

**Ready to design your own
Affinitek and head into battle?**

Create your account today!

SAVE GAME

THE HUB MAP

GAME MANUAL

AFFINITIES AND TEKNIKS

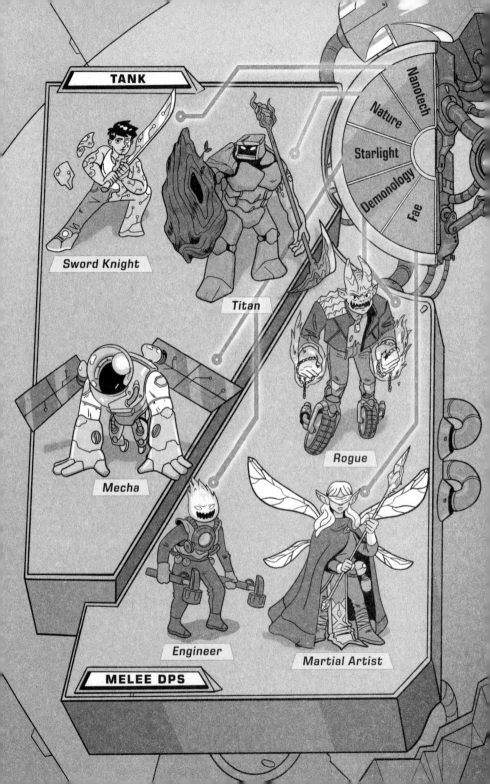

TANK

Sword Knight

Titan

Mecha

Rogue

Engineer

Martial Artist

MELEE DPS

Nanotech

Nature

Starlight

Demonology

Fae

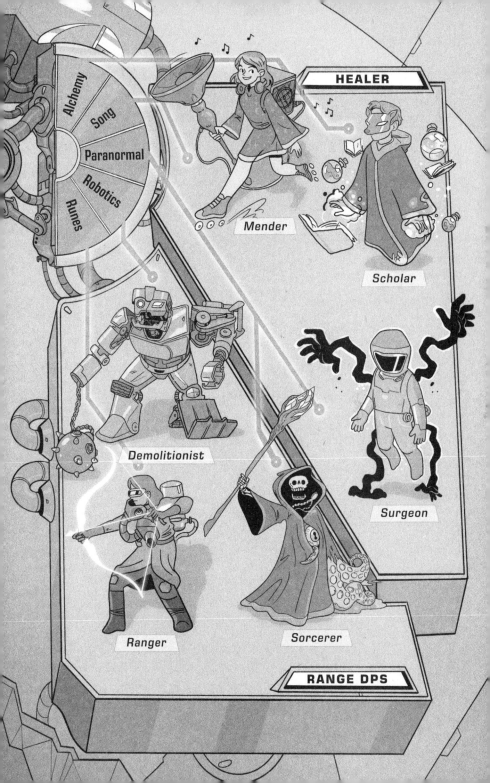